There Once was a Girl from Nantucket

Lori Nayehalski

ISBN: 978-1-80128-078-5

Dedication

To Angel Ed, my insightful father, my guiding light. I am forever indebted to your guidance, encouragement, and infinite love.

May the heavenly stars shine brighter with your presence.

Acknowledgment

I would like to express my special thanks to the following people;

My Dream Team, thank you all for helping me with this soul's journey!

Genevieve, my loving daughter, who always knows the right thing to say at the right time. My daughter, whose insight and angelic presence makes it easy and a delight to be your mother! Thank you for being my earth angel!

Laura, my best friend, who is more like family. Thank you for always listening and offering your solid advice. Thank you for being my unpaid therapist!

Robin, my soul sister, who has graced me with fun and wisdom beyond her own understanding. Thank you for being part of my tribe!

Bentley, my adorable fluffy-toed dog, who brings me safety, security, and peace in the light and darkness.

Saving the best for last; to Angel Ed, my deceased father and guiding light who always looks out for me, protects me, and who always brings the right people into my life. Thank you for being my personal angel!

About the Author

Lori Nayehalski desired a life change. In 2017, when she left her 21-year career in the Natural Gas Industry, moved to Miami, and started her journey to London for screenwriting class.

During that time, her father, Edward, became extremely ill with a rare form of bone cancer. Lori found writing to be her only escape into happiness.

Death knocked on Edward's door suddenly, and he answered it, leaving this life on December 3, 2018. It was a couple of months later that Lori finished writing the screenplay "There Once was a Girl from Nantucket" on February 6, 2019.

It had instantly become such a hit among friends that she knew it needed to be turned into a novel first, before going on the big screen. Lori put this thought on the back burner, considering her continuing need to heal.

Her healing continued, and by her 43rd birthday, she created over 400 paintings in a month and soon turned her artwork into fabric.

Lori was falling in love with becoming a fashion and fabric designer. She felt off balance and asked her Angel, Ed, what direction was next.

A picture arose, and it was her father pointing a finger towards the curtains. She then developed Pearl Edward Home and created curtains. Lori proved her concept and started working with a launch company. However, the price exceeded Lori's resources.

Lori revisited her writing and decided to move to Laguna Beach, California.

Lori and her daughter, Genevieve, have always had a great relationship and treated Covid as a gift and reminder of what was profoundly important to them.

They used to make frequent trips to the beach, but after they closed the beaches, Lori realized she needed to stay creative with her time and energy. She began painting while generating a mass explosion of textile designs for her new artwork, creating a catalog of over 20,000 textile designs.

Soon the beaches reopened, and Lori had a new vision – beach umbrellas.

Lori started Pearl Edward Beach on June 30, 2020, and soon found herself in another holding pattern, knowing her first delivery would not be until the middle of September 2020.

She began tinkering with tie-dye tea towels and soon created Laguna Beach Tie Dye, a beautiful mess. Lori still had the opportunity to be creative with color and now textile again.

During this time, an opportunity to turn "There Once was a Girl from Nantucket" from a screenplay into a novel knocked, and she seized the moment!

Lori found alignment between writing the book, running Pearl Edward Beach, and marketing Laguna Beach Tie-Dye.

During this time-period, Lori worked on keeping her flow open and learned to follow the signs as they presented themselves.

Throughout the ordeals in her life, she was broken. She was, in essence, broken open! Now, she is excited to share with you her youthful romantic modern-day novel and hopes it bring smile on your face!

Preface

There Once was a Girl from Nantucket is a simple modern-day love story. The book will remind you of what it's like to be in love with two people at the same time. With every chapter, follow Ellie on the journey of finding love, tackling tragedies, and taking care of people dearest to her. She spends each day with the people she loves the most. We follow the life of a single mom – Ellie Edward from Nantucket, who is thirty-something, with a comfortable life. Ellie is searching for that missing piece of her puzzle. She is the kind of woman who has never had anything easy, and despite her many struggles, there is one thing she has not given up on yet – LOVE.

Ellie is hopeful that one of these days, her dream man will walk through the door, but what will happen when her dream man turns out to be more than two people? She is caught up when she meets a guy, Drew, who just happens to tick all the boxes and everything in her life starts to make sense...until she unexpectedly meets another man, and with that, her whole life turns upside down. As the story unfolds, Ellie soon learns that not everyone is as honest and simple as they seem.

Contents

Page Left Blank Intentionally

Chapter 1: Pancakes Anyone?

It was a quiet morning with the sun streaming through the window, brilliantly lighting up the beautiful white marbled kitchen. The aroma of fresh pancakes sifted up from the stove and made its way around the house, welcoming a bright new day.

The pattering of feet in the kitchen resounded in the quiet house. I stood by the stove, relishing the serenity that often accompanied the beginning of the day. I played around with the spatula in my hands then put the omelet I had made for myself on a plate. On the other burner, the batter was ready to turn into fluffy chocolate chip pancakes.

I loved coming down for breakfast; it was mainly because I got to spend time in the kitchen. I looked around at my expansive favorite spot in the house, which held a massive island in the center topped with Carrera marble. I had picked out fresh pink flowers this morning and set them in a vase atop the island.

I looked over at the large petals and saw them softly moving with the breeze entering from the open window. My eyes immediately traveled to my daughter, Eva, who sat at the table and was oh-so-focused on coloring the picture of Elsa from Frozen.

Eva bore a striking resemblance to me, especially when it came to attention. Once she put her mind on something, she had to get it done. This time, she was focused on finishing the coloring before she left for school. I smiled as I noted the tinge of golden from the sunlight on her otherwise pale blonde hair.

Everyone said she looked just like me; even her hair was exactly like mine. I smiled.

"How many pancakes would you like, darling?" I called out to her.

"Ummmmm, just two, Mom. One for me and one for Edward," she said, pointing at the fluffy-toed, floppy-eared golden retriever lying beside the chair. Upon hearing his name, Edward lifted his head off the floor. I smiled and turned towards the batter.

"You're so sweet, Eva... Always looking out for your little Edward," I said. I could almost see Edward and Eva look at each other from the corner of my eyes.

"Can you add chocolate chips to mine?" Eva called out.

"Of course, Love Bug. Edward, would you like some peanut butter added to yours?" I asked, then let out a laugh as Edward licked his lip.

"I guess that's a yes," I muttered and added the ingredients to the batter. As the heat rose up from the stove, I reminisced of my dad making me pancakes as a child before he headed to the shelter to help the others. Dad always had a way of making me feel special. As I placed the pancake on Eva's plate, I thought about how I could be a better Mother. I smiled at the thought and carried the pancakes over to Eva and Edward, accompanied by my omelet and juice.

"Are you ready for your first day of school?" I called out. It was a big day for Eva, especially considering how excited she was just last night. As I sat beside her, I saw her look up at me.

"Yes, Mom," she said and rolled her eyes.

"I have everything I need," she said and patted at the backpack sitting next to her at the table. She picked it up and hugged her new bag, excitedly.

"I have my pencils, crayons, notebooks, and that green stuff Gramsey says nobody can live without."

This time, it was me who rolled my eyes.

"Oh yes, you just simply cannot live without the hand sanitizer," I said.

Sarah, my stepmother, was very keen on cleanliness, and sanitizer was probably the first thing she must have told Eva to pack.

"Yes, Mom... and scented lotion too," she chuckled.

"Yes, darling, I understand," I said, fixing her hair. Just then, the cell phone rang, sending a trill of soft tunes around the silent kitchen. Eva immediately hopped from the table and rushed to grab the phone off the countertop.

"It's Gramsey!" she said excitedly and jumped to answer the call. I turned towards the pancakes on the table and felt a sudden rush of sadness make its way to me. I tried to settle it down and turned my attention to Eva instead. She had now sat back down with a big smile on her face.

“Hello, Gramsey!” she said. Sarah was a loud talker, so I could almost hear her through the phone.

“Hello, darling! Are you wicked excited for your first day of school?” she asked, channeling the same energy towards Eva.

“Of course, Gramsey. I can’t wait to try the school lunches. You know how Mom’s cooking is.”

“EVA!" I said sternly, and she chuckled.

“Just kidding, Mom,” she laughed, then put her hand over her mouth as she whispered, “I’m not kidding.”

I smiled and rolled my eyes, then took a sip of juice.

“I know, darling, I know,” Gramsey Sarah said.

I looked up at Eva again as she spoke.

“Is that Gramps? Can I say hi to him?” she asked eagerly. I guess she must have heard him in the background. Eva put him on speaker and then set the phone down as she rushed into the kitchen to get a glass of water. Gramps coughed loudly and then cleared his throat.

“Good Morning, my little sugar dumpling smarty pants,” he said with a snicker, trying to bury a new wave of cough erupting through him.

“Knock em’ dead, kiddo!” he said and then was overcome by a fresh round of coughs. He was struggling to stop it, but he couldn't. I watched my daughter's bright, hopeful eyes turn concerned and slowly mask the same sadness I felt.

"Gramps, are you OK?” she asked softly.

“Oh yes, Dumpling. I am great! I am so proud of you,” he said happily. Eva smiled, but it didn’t reach her eyes.

“Thank you, Gramps,” she said and heard him begin to cough again. Quickly, my stepmother took over the call, and I was so thankful.

"Gramps?" Eva asked.

"He's OK, Eva. You have an amazing first-day, little girl!" Gramsey said quickly and reassuringly.

"Thanks, Gramsey. Ciao."

"Ciao," she said, and the line went dead. I remained silent and then slowly pushed the plate towards Eva. Together, we ate breakfast, not wanting to bring up the conversation again.

Once we had finished our food, I picked up the plates and placed them in the sink.

"Alright, hurry up and pack up. We need to take first-day pictures as well. Chop chop!" I said as I noticed Eva was picking up another colored pencil again.

"Just one last color, mom! Just... one... done!" she said and picked up her book to show me.

"Oh, that is so pretty. She has your eyes," I said and lightly pinched Eva's nose. Eva chuckled and quickly picked up her bag. She had chirped up again, and I was glad she was now looking forward to school once again.

I rushed upstairs to grab my bag and shoes, but my eyes got caught by the picture on my side table. It was a picture of my dad holding Eva, and he looked so healthy and happy. I almost couldn't believe it was him. Dad's health had deteriorated so quickly that now even he feared for it.

I sat on the bed and picked up the picture, smiling at how happy he looked with not a care in the world.

"Mom! You're going to make me late!" I heard Eva call, and suddenly, I came back to reality again. I quickly placed the picture down and rushed out of my room. I checked the stove then led Eva out the door.

"Oh, I almost forgot!" I said and rushed inside to pick up the drawings I had made for Eva. I quickly picked up the keys from the key holder near the door and then stepped out into the summer heat.

Our eyes strained at the bright sun shining down on us, and I put my sunglasses on immediately. Once I locked my house, I turned around. I had carefully chosen this house because of how beautiful it was.

It was a large, old, traditional style, Nantucket mansion with fall mums lining the steps. Right in front of me, the steps paved the way to a large circular hydrangea bush right in the middle of the driveway. The white gates in the distance were surrounded by the luscious green of trees.

I looked up at the bright sky and noticed how the clouds passed over us in unison, so calmly. My attention went back to the soft crunches of footsteps against the driveway, and I looked for little Eva lugging a bag that seemed to be twice her size. She had picked it out especially for today and was a little too excited for it.

As I looked at her, I realized that I was more excited than Eva was because I saw her making her way to the SUV with Edward in tow.

“One picture before we get on the road. Here, I made you a sign,” I said quickly, picking up one of the little drawings from beside the door.

“Mom!” Eva whined, but I wasn’t going to let my daughter go off to first grade without a picture!

“Just one. How about two? One with you and Edward,” I pleaded.

“OK, Mom. Come on, Edward. Let’s get this over with,” she sighed and walked over to the front porch.

“Success!” I thought to myself and rushed over to position myself for the perfect picture. They were all turning out great. The light was perfect, the background perfectly complimented Eva’s clothes, and it created a vibe of happiness, just as I wanted it to.

I quickly took one picture of Eva and Edward then ran in for one with me in it too. Eva held the sign I had made, which read, "FIRST GRADE 2019," and then stuck out her tongue. In the next picture, she held up the peace sign while Edward sat properly, looking up at Eva.

I smiled at the pictures and looked at Eva one more time. I promised myself I wouldn't cry, but I couldn't help it. I couldn't believe she was growing up so fast! Before she could see the tears in my eyes, I turned around and clapped my hands.

"Great job, guys! Let's get this show on the road!" I said happily.

Eva rolled her eyes and walked over to the slick, black Range Rover. I opened the door for her and Edward. Edward got in front, as usual, while Eva sat in the back. Those were their designated spots from the very beginning, of course, because Eva had been much too young to sit in the front seat. I closed the doors then headed over to my side. As soon as I got in, I put the seatbelt on, started the ignition, and then took a deep breath.

"Alright guys, are you ready?" I asked.

"Let's go!" Eva called out. I turned on the radio and turned to see her dancing to the music. I laughed and drove to school.

Chapter 2: Coffee Shopping

I stopped outside of The Bean after tearfully dropping Eva off and wishing her good luck on her first day. She was pretty excited, but it was still quite emotional for me. I could hardly believe my little girl was growing up so fast!

I sighed as I saw people walking into the small coffeehouse for their morning coffee. None of the other stores surrounding it was open yet. As I turned off the ignition, I turned to Edward. He was already getting restless at the sight of a squirrel that had passed by.

"Hold on, Edward. I'll get the door," I told him as he whined. He truly was our overgrown baby! I got off and stepped over to his side. I opened the door, immediately seeing the golden ball of fur jump out and rush towards one of the trees. Defeated, he sauntered back to me.

"Let's grab a snack, Edward," I said and quickly closed the door to follow him inside. I was greeted by the soft ding and the smell of fresh coffee.

"Edward, stay by me, sweetie," I said and snapped my fingers, a command that he was used to. He walked by me, and I grabbed hold of his leash. Thankfully, the queue wasn't too long.

With the soft hum of music in the background and the chatter of people lounging out on the brown leather chairs with their laptops, newspapers, or friends, I suddenly felt happy. I looked around at jars lining the shelves behind the counter. The tiny little shop was laden with tables and chairs by the walls. The Bean was my happy place, and it was mostly because of the ambiance.

As the woman in front of me placed her order and moved, I stepped forward and scanned the menu on the counter. I looked up to meet the cashier's friendly smile.

"Good Morning, What can I get yah?" she asked.

"Good Morning. I would like a quad shot of espresso and a piece of that beautiful banana bread," I said, eyeing the bread placed in glass cake-holders on the counter. My eyes went to Edward, who was licking his lips.

"Gorgeous," I heard someone mutter behind me, and I turned to meet a brawny younger man with dirty blonde hair and gorgeous green eyes.

"Excuse me?" I asked, keeping my voice firm. It was as though he was lost in a trance. He suddenly zoned back to reality and became serious.

"Wow... must be a rough morning?" he said.

I couldn't help it; I smirked.

"First day of school. Big First Grader, big day for my daughter," I said.

He smiled.

"Oh, mine as well. I'm Drew," he said, extending his hand. "Our kids must be in the same class. My son's name is Curtis."

I shook his hand and smiled back at him.

"Oh, too funny. Nice to meet you. I'm Ellie, and my daughter's name is Eva."

"Nice to see you. I mean… meet you." He chuckled nervously. It was kind of cute. The cashier cleared her throat and smirked knowingly to herself.

"What can I get started for yah?" she asked Drew.

Undoubtedly, Drew was quite a charmer and not too bad in the looks department either. He held my gaze for a moment too long, smiled, and then turned towards the woman working the counter. Yep, that did it! I glanced at his hands, noticing no wedding band on his finger.

Score.

"Yes, thank you, I would like the same thing she is having, but substitute the banana bread for that Pumpkin Chocolate Chip Croissant."

I turned around and grabbed a seat by one of the windows where Edward was already leading me.

"Would you like to join us?" I asked Drew.

"Sure!"

Together we grabbed a seat.

"This is Edward," I said. The golden retriever immediately perked up at the mention of his name. Drew looked at him, kneeled, and then began to pet him.

"Nice to meet you, Edward," he said and held out his hand. Eva and I had worked hard to train him, and now he would shake hands almost immediately. I smiled proudly as the dog placed his paw into Drew's hands.

"Wow! He's smart and polite," he laughed, then stood up.

"He was raised right. Edward is our sweet cutie bear." Edward looked up at me. I sat down with Drew on the opposite side. The sun was streaming in and falling onto the side of his face, bringing a sparkle to his eyes.

"How's this spot?" he asked as he positioned his chair away from the sun.

"Perfect!"

As Drew relaxed in his seat, Edward walked over and lay down beside his chair. What a traitor!

"Really, Edward?" I said in mock disbelief.

"I guess he likes me." Drew smiled, immediately making me blush. I turned away quickly, hoping he didn't see the red creeping to my cheeks.

"Yes, I guess he does."

"Ellie, I haven't seen you around the island. Did you just move here?" Drew asked, looking intently at me.

"Yes, but I was born here. We just moved back from Boston. I needed a fresh start, and I always loved Nantucket. So, we moved back."

Drew nodded and then smiled in understanding.

"We did the same thing. My father and younger brother live here. A fresh start is always a good idea," he said, picking up his cup and taking a sip of his espresso.

"Interesting," I said, taking a sip of mine.

"Everything happens for a reason, Ellie," Drew said, and there was something in his eyes that made me understand what he meant.

"I totally agree, Drew."

Just then, my phone dinged, and the little bar showed the Bumble icon.

"Someone on Bumble likes you (besides us – we love you!) Aren't you curious to know who? Swipe to see if it's a match!"

I quickly turned to Drew and locked eyes with him, then slowly flipped my phone over so I didn't have to see the screen. He was not stupid; the tone is pretty specific to Bumble, so he probably figured it out. I adjusted in my seat and smiled sweetly at him.

"So, Drew. What do you do for a living?"

"I am a Website Designer," he told me, and I couldn't believe my luck.

"Oh, cool. I might need your help in the near future. I'm working on a startup called Pearl Edward Beauty. It is a line of Sugar Scrub and Epsom Salts. It's just in the product development stages at present," I said.

Drew was evidently intrigued because his face lit up, and then he began rummaging through his pockets. Finally, he took out his wallet, opened it, and took out a business card.

"Yes, absolutely. I love sugar scrubs! Here's my business card," he said, handing it over to me. I had yet to come across men who liked sugar scrubs, so you can imagine my surprise. I'm sure he was bluffing, but he looked pretty serious.

"You do?" I asked him.

He smiled, then leaned in as if he was going to tell me a secret.

"That's how I keep my skin so soft and young-looking. Don't tell anyone." He winked.

I giggled. He really was a charmer. I noticed how, very quietly; he was inching just a little bit closer to me.

"So what do you do in your spare time?" he asked as he bit into his croissant.

"Let's see. Spare time. What is spare time?" I chuckled.

“Any hobbies?” he asked, and I was suddenly very self-conscious. Regardless, I didn’t see the harm in sharing it. I took a sip of espresso and sat back.

“Yoga. I do Yoga. And I read. Let’s see...I also take long walks on the beach, meditate, and I enjoy cooking and help run my family’s foundation,” I said.

“Yoga. Interesting.”

“I know. I know. I’m kind of boring.” I giggled.

“Not at all. I enjoy all those things as well. Well, not the cooking, but I love eating.”

I laughed a little louder than I would have liked.

“I’m a pretty good cook, if I do say so myself,” I said and watched as Edward lifted his head in protest. Oh, what did he know?

“And the foundation is pretty amazing. We help homeless people get back on their feet," I told Drew, and he seemed impressed.

“That is extremely commendable.”

“Thank you! Our family is very proud to be able to give back,” I told him.

“I love hearing stories of people helping other people. So you are generous, humble, and gorgeous!”

“Thank you, Drew darling,” I said and felt another blush creep up. I didn’t shy away this time. There was something enchanting about him. I maintained eye contact with him as I munched on the last bite of the bread.

Another ding from my phone caught my attention, and, as though breaking away from a pull, I turned away and picked up my phone. It was my contractor’s appointment in an hour, and I still needed to do my daily beach mediation. I stood up and smiled as I wrapped Edward's leash around my hand.

He stood up as well.

“Well, it was very nice to meet you, Drew.”

“You, as well, gorgeous. I look forward to seeing you again,” Drew said.

"Come on, Edward," I said, gently nudging him. The dog ambled over to my side. Together, we headed out the door.

As I sat in the car and put on my seat belt, my eyes wandered over to the window where Drew was seated. I could see him sitting there with headphones on, bobbing his head as he opened his laptop. Edward whined, and I looked at him.

"I know, I know. We're leaving." I petted him, smiled, and drove off.

Chapter 3: Beach Bum Meditation

The sun shined brilliantly in the sky, illuminating the green of Nantucket. It was the perfect weather for the beach. I stepped out of the car and heard the sounds of the waves splashing across the shore.

I usually came at this time, so I could enjoy nothing but the sounds of water overlapping the sands. The gentle breeze across my face was refreshing, but it was Edward who always looked forward to it the most. He absolutely loved the beach, and he was the reason I had made it a habit to come here in the first place.

I walked over to the back of the car and took out a towel. Edward stayed by my side as I walked towards the water, often standing to glance up at me as if saying thank you. The sand stuck to his fur, but that was the part he loved the most.

I covered my eyes, looked up at a bird flying across the sky, and then glanced at my watch.

"Well, Edward, it looks like we have an hour before our roofing appointment. Let's meditate," I said. He whined but followed me regardless.

I set the towel down at my favorite spot then got into position. I often let Edward free. He never really left my side for too long; he would always return after one or two dips in the water.

I closed my eyes and allowed myself to focus on the soft splashes of water. I took a deep breath... one in, then one out. I felt the wind across my face and then...hot, panting breath?

I felt a dog sniffing me, and before I could react, I felt the hot spray of piss right on my back. I fell onto the sand and stood up immediately to see a little dog standing there.

"NOOOOOOOOOOOOOOOOOOOOOOOOOOOOOO! Bad dog! Bad dog! Oh, God!" I shouted, but before I could chase it away, a man came running up to me, trying to catch the dog's leash.

"Jesus! STOP, Mr. Pickles! Bad Pickles! I am so sorry, lady!" he said, and it sounded so ridiculous, I couldn't stop the laughter that left my throat.

Next thing I knew, I had forgotten about the piss and was laughing loud about the fact that the dog's name was Mr. Pickles.

"Mr. Pickles? Mr. Pickles? You named your dog Mr. Pickles?" I laughed.

"Yes. I love pickles," the man said earnestly, putting an abrupt stop to my laughter. I cleared my throat and then looked at the dog as he looked up innocently at me.

"Thanks for the golden shower, Mr. Pickles!" I said. Just then, the man turned to me as if he was only just noticing that I was a person standing here. He took his glasses off and placed them on top of his head. He starred into Ellie's stunning blue eyes for a moment and became instantly captivated.

"I am so sorry. Can I get you out of these clothes and wash them for you? Or buy you a coffee or dinner?" he asked in a soft voice.

"Anything to apologize for Mr. Pickles." He tugged gently on the leash, and the dog bowed his head sadly.

"Mr. Pickles, just don't let it happen again."

I shook my finger at the dog then bent to pick up my towel.

"I have to get going. I have a roofing appointment," I said. The man now looked surprised, and I could not fathom why.

"Jesus...Noelle?" he asked.

Now, I was officially creeped out. Not only did a stranger's dog piss on me, but this guy also knew my name.

"How did you know my name?"

"I'm Jack, your roofer," he said, and I shook my head in disbelief. What a coincidence!

I smiled and shook his hand.

"Nice to meet you, Jack."

Chapter 4: Falling In Love

It was a beautiful morning, and while the incident at the beach did somewhat gross me out, it didn't really take away from the essence of the day. I got out of the Range Rover and saw Jack parking his F350 right behind me. He got out and smiled, then looked towards the house.

"I'm going to grab the ladder and head up on that roof. I should be able to put together that estimate for you tonight since you are my VIP Customer," he said. I could not help but be confused.

"VIP?" I asked.

"Yes, I kind of owe you one, don't you think?"

"Absolutely!" I laughed as he covered his eyes with shame. It was cute, really.

"I will be inside getting changed if you need anything."

I headed into the house as he grabbed his ladder and placed it against the wall. I was already in my room by now, taking off my clothes to get into something more comfortable, when suddenly, I heard a loud clink of metal followed by Edward's incessant barks. Alarmed, I threw on my clothes and rushed downstairs to see Edward barking at the foot of the stairs. He seemed so frantic, it worried me.

"What is it, boy?" I asked, and just then, I heard Jack's screams.

"JESUS! HELP! HELP ME, NOELLE! HELP!" Edward rushed out, looking back now and then to see if I was following. I rushed through the open door, almost tripping over the fallen ladder. Jack was just a short distance away, sprawled over the floor with blood gushing from the arm he held tightly.

"JESUS! HELP!" he shouted, then saw me rushing toward him. I was so panicked that I couldn't really understand what was going on.

"Oh my God, do I need to call an ambulance?" I asked, but Jack quickly shook his head.

“No, no, just help me up?” He winced as he extended his good arm. Now that I saw he wasn’t as hurt as I had initially thought, I couldn’t help but stare at him and then narrow my eyes at him flirtatiously.

"Looks like you've fallen for me, Jack." I giggled, and Jack smirked. His hair was disheveled, and he looked cute. What else was I supposed to do?

“Jesus, Noelle, this is no time for jokes!” he said as I helped him on his feet. He stumbled and almost fell onto me but quickly caught his balance. There was a silence that stretched between us for a couple of seconds before the pain interrupted whatever was happening between us and made him fall back and wince.

"How do you feel now?" I asked, concerned. It was evident that he was biting back a groan, but he took a deep breath and then looked at the red staining his arm.

“I think I am OK, but can you run me over to the emergency room?"

“Absolutely! Let me just get my keys.” I said, rushing inside and picking them up before disappearing out again.

Chapter 5: Hospital

I never really liked hospitals. It was always the nauseating antiseptic smell that got to me, but mostly, it was the surroundings. There was always a kind of sadness in the air that I never liked. As I sat in the emergency room, I noticed how quiet it was, contrary to what they often showed in movies.

It was spotless, too – the white sparkling floors and walls complemented the black seats and brown, polished furniture. My eyes then traveled to Jack, who had walked up to the reception and was signing some forms.

Even as he stood there with an injured arm, I could see the aura of confidence surrounding him. He was undoubtedly charming, and it seemed like he knew it. My eyes traveled to the clock right above the receptionist's desk, and I realized I had to leave for Eva. I should inform him first.

I picked up a magazine and was fanning through the pages when I heard him approaching me. He sat down and let out a loud sigh, just as I got up.

"I hate to leave you like this, but I need to go and pick up my daughter from school," I said and eyed his arm.

"You sure you're alright?" I asked him.

"Oh, yeah. It's no problem, I completely understand. Thank you for helping me," he smiled.

"Anytime. By the way, I expect that roof completed by Halloween with a discount from Mr. Pickles." I giggled. Jack smiled and pretended to salute.

"AYE, AYE Captain! I've already texted one of my guys. He should have your estimate and discount up for you before your morning coffee. We should be able to start within the next two weeks. Your roof will definitely be finished by Halloween," he said.

No doubt, I was impressed. All of it was done without my asking, and quite fast as well. I turned and headed for the door.

"BYE BYE, Captain Jack!" I called and then walked out.

Chapter 6: Pick Up Line

I drove towards the school, leaving all thoughts of Jack back at the hospital with him. I passed by a few cars and finally pulled up at the school's entrance. My eyes immediately landed on Eva standing amongst other kids and teachers, her hair flying as she hopped toward the car. I smiled and waved to her.

“How was your first day, darling?" I asked as soon as she sat in the backseat. Her eyes scanned the car, and then she looked at me with confusion.

“Good, Mom. Where's Edward?”

“He's at home, honey. I had a little bit of a change of plans for today,” I told her as I began to drive off.

“Why's that, mom?”

I smiled and glanced at her from the rearview mirror and then focused back on the road.

“Oh, honey, big kid problems,” I said, smiling to myself as I thought of Jack again.

“OK, Mom,” she said, and then I heard the movement of the seat as she leaned forward excitedly.

"School was cool. We did painting, snack time, recess, lunch, and looked at the map of the world." Eva's voice picked up, and before I knew it, she was telling me everything that had happened. Her excitement made me excited too.

“That's amazing!”

“Mom, do you know some of these kids have never left the island?” Eva said in disbelief.

“Yes, honey.” I laughed.

“I shared it with the class. I told them that the fresh pasta in Italy is to die for.”

“Oh, good, honey!” I said and immediately thought of Drew. I glanced at Eva again.

"Oh, by the way, did you meet a little boy named Curtis today?" I asked her.

"He goes by Curt, Mom," she replied, and immediately I perked up.

"Excuse me?"

"He is silly. He sits next to me. He likes these things called Pokémon cards. Have you ever heard of such a thing?" she said with horror, making me laugh.

"I don't know anything about them. I was raised on Garbage Pail kids," I smiled.

"Garbage Pail Kids? What the-"

"EVA!" I almost shouted when I saw her raise her arms up in surrender.

"Sorry, Mom! But what on earth are Garbage Pail kids?"

"Cards that I used to collect and share with my friends," I told her.

"Cool, Mom. Can you show me when we get home?" she asked, her voice so innocent I couldn't deny it.

"If I can find them, I will," I told her, and then her head popped up from between the front seats.

"Hey, Mom! Can we watch the Sox game and grab a pizza?"

"Get out of my head, girl! I was just going to ask you the same question. What kind of pizza?" I asked her excitedly and could see her eyes widen and then glimmer with excitement.

"MOM! You know!"

I shook my head and took a turn.

"Silly me! Pineapple and ham, right?" I said.

"Hawaiian! Always a good reminder of Auntie in Maui."

"Always!" I smiled. I pulled up in the driveway and heard the ring of my phone. As soon as I picked it up, I was greeted by Simone's picture smiling back at me. I turned back to Eva.

“Speak of the devil," I said, and she grabbed the phone from my hands and then hopped out. I got out of the car and followed her towards the house, seeing Edward barking excitedly through the window from the lounge.

“AUNTIE!” Eva said excitedly. "AUNTIE! I better be your favorite! I'm your only one!" I heard Eva say, and I smiled as we entered the house.

I sat on the sofa with Eva right opposite to me, and Edward came running in.

“We did painting! And I even taught my new friend, Nicole Two, how to do downward dog at recess! Just like you taught me… Yes, auntie, Nicole Two. Her mother’s name is Nicole. So she said her name is Nicole Two. You know... Like the Incredibles and the Incredibles 2.”

I smiled, listening to my daughter's narration of her day at school.

Eva nodded solemnly to what Simone said on the other side and continued, “I thought it was interesting too. I also have a boy and his uncle in my class. Yes, his name is Curt, and his uncle’s name is Daniel, but we call him Danny.”

With Edward constantly bugging her to pet him, Eva quickly tightened her grip on the phone. I stood up and walked into the kitchen; Eva’s voice was dimming with the distance.

“Hey, Auntie! We just got home, and I need to give Edward a big hug and tell him about my day. Can I have mom call you back? I LOVE YOU, AUNTIE! Sayonara!” she said, and then I heard her talking to Edward and hugging him. She followed shortly after, taking off her bag and placing it on the counter. Together, we began to unpack her things and put them back in their place.

“How is Auntie doing?” I asked her.

“Good, Mom. I told her you would call her back after we got settled in the house.”

“Thank you, honey." I smiled and took the phone from her. I dialed Simone's number, and when I looked up, Eva was already occupied with coloring once again.

“Aloha!” Simone’s cheerful voice greeted me as soon as the call connected.

“Aloha! How are you doing?”

"Doing OK. Ellie, I need to talk to you about something." Her tone became serious, and I grew worried. Simone was hardly ever serious, and when she was, it meant it was important. I grabbed a seat and turned away from Eva.

"Are you OK?" I asked.

“Yes, but Dad is not,” she said, and I took a deep breath. “Dad had been ill for quite some time, and my worries had grown even more after listening to him today.”

“I know. I heard him this morning,” I told Simone.

“Sarah called and said that Dad wants to start looking into hospice services.”

There was a silence that occupied the house this time, a kind of darkness that I couldn't deny. I felt the tears begin to form and slowly roll down my cheeks. I had always seen dad as the strong, healthy one. To witness the condition that he had now reached absolutely tore me apart.

“Well... we knew the time was coming,” I said, but I was not prepared for it.

“Yes. It doesn’t make it any easier,” Simone said.

“No, it doesn’t,” I whispered. The silence between us stretched, each of us lost in our own thoughts. I didn’t know what else I could say; the last thing I needed was to let Simone in on my own sadness about the situation.

“I’m going to make plans to head to Boston in a few days,” she said, and it got me thinking.

“Sounds good. I will head that way this weekend and see you there,” I said finally.

“Love you, Mahalo.”

“Love you,” I said and let my hands slip onto my lap. I kept looking at it for a while, then slowly stood up, grabbed a tissue, and headed to the bathroom. I let myself drown in the memories of dad, how he always put his kids' interests before his own, took us for ice cream whenever we asked, and then got scolded by mom.

I looked around the bathroom, listened to the birds chirping outside, and sat on the toilet, letting myself wallow in the inevitable pain. I allowed myself to cry and release the sadness and worry I kept in me for so long. I dabbed my eyes with a tissue and then cried until I heard the soft scratches on the bathroom door. I sniffed and opened it, allowing Edward to rush inside.

Like the sensible, faithful dog that he was, Edward remained still and placed his head on my lap for comfort. I smiled and put my hand on his head, slowly tousling his soft fur.

"Oh Edward, you are my sweet little angel," I said and sat there for a while longer.

Nothing could save me from what I was feeling now; the emptiness within me only grew. I gathered myself and stood up, taking a deep breath. My eyes traveled to my reflection, and I daubed my eyes with a damp tissue to diminish the after-effects of crying. Once I was convinced I looked all right, I headed out with Edward in tow.

Eva was still coloring and definitely waiting for me to order the pizza. The first thing I did was grab a bottle of wine, pour a large glass for myself, and then sit down with my phone.

"Yes, I would like a large thin crust Hawaiian pizza delivered to 123 Pine Street. Thank you," I said and then cut the call. It was a long way to go for the weekend, and I couldn't wait.

It was only a little while later that my thoughts were disrupted by the doorbell. Eva stood up and rushed towards it, with Edward barking and following her. I rushed to grab my wallet.

"PIZZA IS HERE, MOM!"

"I'm on my way!" I called and then walked towards the door with a $50 bill in hand. I loved how Edward stood there eagerly, a string of drool escaping his lips at the aroma of pizza.

"That will be $21.21 plus $3.33 delivery charges," the delivery guy said, and I handed him the note.

“Here you go, son. Keep the change," I said and smiled as his eyes widened with happiness.

“OH, MAN! THANK YOU SO MUCH! THANK YOU! THANK YOU!” he kept on repeating. It was wholesome, but it made me sad, thinking of how dad would do the same sometimes.

“Thank you, have a good night!”

“You too, Miss,” he said happily as I shut the door.

“Pizza bones for Edward!” Eva called out and ran to the kitchen with Edward rushing there too, wagging his tail. I guess he understood what she said.

I walked into the living room and turned on the baseball game, pouring myself another large glass of wine. Right beside the TV was a shelf with photo frames and decoration pieces. I glanced at the picture of dad in a Red Sox cap, once again bringing me close to tears.

Ellie rushed in with the pizza and joined me. We snuggled together and enjoyed the best we could as I once again fell into the memories of dad.

Chapter 7: Darkness Arrives

I dreamt of nothing, but it really wasn't just nothing. There was a sound in the distance, and it slowly kept on inching closer. I couldn't tell what it was, but the sound got louder and louder, then finally....

My eyes fluttered open to the loud ringing of my phone, and when I glanced at the screen, Sarah's name was on it. A sense of dread filled me as I looked at the time; it was 3 AM. I sat up and switched on the light.

“Sarah... What is it?” I asked, trying to calm myself. Her voice cracked, and she was sobbing.

“Noelle, it’s your father. He died,” she said. All the sleep left me, and I felt the blood drain from my body. I sat there with the phone in my hands in stunned silence.

"He was coughing real bad. I called 911... it all happened so fast. They came as quick as they could, but..." Her voice trailed off, and now I began to sob as well. I grabbed the tissue and blew into it, but nothing could stop the tears. Edward was on alert now, moving closer to me.

“I’m sorry, Noelle,” Sarah cried, and it was then that I could feel my voice returning to me.

“I’m sorry, too. I will call you back later, Sarah,” I said and ended the call. I lay in bed and snuggled next to Edward.

"Oh, Edward. He was my best friend. My favorite person! What am I going to do without him?" I whispered and held him tighter. I sobbed softly as I felt the immense loss. He was gone, taking a part of me with him. I got up and texted my best friend, Lola.

“Call me when you wake up or get home. I need you!” I wrote and then slowly rolled out of bed. The house was exceptionally quiet and empty as I made my way downstairs into the kitchen.

The bright light in the kitchen came on, and I made myself a double shot of espresso. I felt numb, and I didn't even understand what I was doing. I felt like a zombie, with my legs having a mind of their own.

Intense sadness filled me, and no matter how much coffee I drank, it wasn't enough. I grabbed a box of tissues, went to the living room, and grabbed a picture of my dad in a red sox cap. I traced his face with my finger and the lines of his smile. He was always so happy, and now he was just...gone.

The silence was disturbed by Lola's call.

"Hi," I said.

"YO! What are you doing up at this hour?"

"Not partying like you," I tried to be amusing but failed.

"Hehehe! How did you know I was just getting home?"

"I know you like the back of my hand."

"Yes, indeed. Are you OK?"

"No. I need you to come to Nantucket immediately," I said, looking at dad's picture.

"What!"

"My father just died. Sarah just called," I said. Even saying it felt wrong, like it wasn't actually real.

"What! Oh, Sweets, I'm on my way!" she said.

I walked back to the kitchen to add some Bailey's into the espresso. I wanted something strong, something to help me, but as I looked at the drink, I realized something. This isn't what dad wanted from me. I poured the drink down the sink and looked at Edward.

"It's time to grow up, Edward," I said and headed upstairs.

Chapter 8: Home Sweet Home

There was silence around the house, and sadness gripped all of our hearts. Me, Eva, Lola, Simone, and Edward were gathered on the oversized u-shaped sofas. An ominous feeling surrounded us. I felt as though we were all bound by the same grief, feeling it in very different ways, even Edward.

I listened to the silence, hoping to hear dad's voice just one last time or see a younger, healthier version of him pop up and tell us it was all an elaborate prank. Alas, this was real, and reality was always harsh.

The silence was broken by the squeak of the leather as Eva moved forward. She grabbed a piece of chocolate from a large bowl on the coffee table. The wrapper sounded much louder than usual. She popped the chocolate in her mouth as she leaned back.

"I'm going to miss Gramps. He always had candy in his pockets for me," she said, her voice cracking a little. I smiled at her and put my hand on her head as she snuggled next to me. I could sense Lola looking at me, and I looked up to meet her eyes.

"I'm going to miss his 'Looney Hill' comments," Lola said, making Simone chuckle. Lola and dad always got along, and she loved spending time with him every time she came over.

"I'm going to miss his Polish meatballs," Simone added. Ah, his Polish meatballs were famous everywhere; no one could have enough of them!

"I'm going to miss his Young and the Restless updates...." I said, making everyone laugh. I looked over at Simone and smiled.

"Don't worry, Simone. Dad taught me how to make the Polish meatballs. It's the one thing I'm good at cooking," I said.

"Will you teach me?"

I could almost hear the pleading in her voice. I felt the same. "Of course. Is tomorrow too soon?"

As soon as I said it, I saw the smile light up on Lola's face. She loved Polish meatballs the most.

"A girl's gotta eat, you know! I love you Polish girls! Best Polish food in town! You always come up with the best ideas." She laughed excitedly.

"I want to help! I love cooking! And my mom's meatballs are the best! I will get my apron ready!" Eva squealed. I couldn't believe how something so small could suddenly lighten everyone's mood. Dad's famous Polish meatballs became the talk of the evening then, making everyone come alive and become a little bit happier.

However, the sense of loss still lingered in the air. I took a deep breath and stood up. Edward was getting anxious, so I gestured at him to follow me out for one last pee of the night. He perked up too, jumping off the sofa, wagging his tail.

"Ok, girls. Let's get ready for bed. We have a big day tomorrow." I sighed.

"Sounds good, Mom. I'm sleeping with Auntie tonight!"

"Sounds good, Buttercup." Simone tousled her hair.

"I get the other guest room," Lola announced.

Edward was already in the garden doing his business. I looked around the house, feeling the intense sadness eating away at me. I ignored it for now and walked to the kitchen to let Edward back in. He zoomed past me towards Eva. I smiled and looked up at the women gathered outside the kitchen.

"Good Night, ladies! See you in the morning! Hugs and love all around!" I announced, making everyone walk up to me with their arms. I loved being a part of the group hug; it made me feel complete.

Edward kept running around the group as we broke apart. Eva, Simone, and Lola headed up the staircase, leaving me alone once again. I closed the kitchen lights then let my eyes wander to dad's picture one last time.

"Goodnight dad, I hope you're watching over us," I whispered, then turned to the staircase, letting Edward follow me.

Chapter 9: Grocery Store

I wheeled the cart from the stand and turned to see Eva and Lola catching up to us. Simone had grabbed a cart as well and was wheeling it next to me. It was a bright, sunny day, but I felt this emptiness in me that I'm sure was shared by everyone else.

Dad leaving us had hit us all hard. I tried my best not to think about it, but every now and then, I was right there again, missing him.

"Let's split up. I will grab the polish meatball ingredients and junk food," I said as we entered, the soft ding ringing from the entrance. The store was relatively quieter than usual. There was no hubbub of shoppers trying to find everything on the grocery list.

"Sounds good. I will take Eva and head to the organics. I need my special protein shakes to keep my body regular," Simone said.

"Wonderful." I looked around at the aisles.

"YOU KNOW IT!!" Simone replied with a little more energy.

"Let's see what organics they have for kids, Auntie." Eva jumped up and pulled Simone's hand.

"PURRRRFECT!"

"Hey Eva, I'll pick up the Doritos," Lola called out.

"AWESOME! Don't forget the onion dip!" Eva said, and then the girls split up.

Lola and I walked into the fruit section, our eyes scanning through the various lines of red, orange, and green. I picked up a plastic bag and put some apples in it. When I turned to Lola, she looked straight at me with a smirk as she rubbed a banana around her mouth.

"El, look at these bananas. Don't they look delicious? MMMMMMMMMMMMMM!" she said, and I quickly looked around, chuckling as I reached out to her. I sure hoped no one saw!

"Oh my god! Lola, put that down," I whispered fiercely, trying to control my laugh.

"Don't you miss the Banana?"

"It hasn't been that long." I rolled my eyes at her.

"Bitch, please! It's been long enough!" Lola waved the banana at my face one last time before she put it back. I chuckled and shook my head.

"Well... I did meet someone a few weeks ago." I glanced at her mischievously and continued to the vegetable section as if it were nothing. I could hear Lola gasp and rush up to me. I picked up an eggplant and bagged it, chuckling at her.

"See, now you made me hungry for eggplant," I said.

"And...when you say you met someone...did you actually talk to someone or just text him from an online dating app?" Lola pushed, and I looked at her.

"Yes... I met him. His name is Drew. We had coffee together. Our kids are the same age, and most importantly, he appears to be single," I said and saw Lola smiling like a teenager.

"Soooo... when's your second date? You know your dad always wanted you to be happy and to find love again!"

"I don't know," I replied because, honestly, I didn't know. I hadn't had time to think about it.

"What do you mean you don't know?" Lola came and stood in front of me, blocking my path.

"He's young," I said as I scanned through the other greens, missing out on Lola's eyes widening enough to pop out of her head.

"HOW YOUNG? Like Santiago young? The pro golfer from Columbia young?"

Oh, now she did it. I put my hands over my eyes and tossed my head back with a smile on my face.

"He was amazing..." I said as my mind went back to the hunk of a man I had once dated with luxurious curly brown hair and the perfect brown eyes and lips to match. Quickly, I realized where I was and composed myself, looking at Lola.

"No, I'm not doing that again. I would say he's early thirties, very sexy, thick hair, green eyes, taller than me with a raspy voice, straight up sexy – like, Jude Law daddy sexy." I paused and looked at her seriously.

"I don't think it would ever work out," I said simply, moving on.

"Wait, what?! Jude Daddy Law from the Holiday kind of sexy?" she all but shouted, and I nodded.

"Exactly!"

"What! Are you crazy! If you don't date him, I'm going to find him on this island and date him myself!" she said.

"No...No... No..."

"Ok. Ok. What do you mean it would never work? You will never know if you don't go out with him. What if he's the best lay of your life? And you are just going to throw out the best lay of your life? Who does that? Nobody, that's who!" she said, walking with me. Well, the girl wasn't wrong here, I had to admit.

"Well, if you put it like that... Maybe I should explore him a little more." I smirked at her.

"You know those 30-year-olds full of blow and ready to go with typically no emotional baggage. I mean, unless his ex left him for a woman or she died... and then you have a whole other set of issues on your hands," she said, just as my phone dinged. Well, wouldn't you know? It was a text from none other than Drew.

"Hey, Ellie! I was just thinking about you. I would love to see you again and maybe go for a ride on my sailboat," I read out loud and almost burst out laughing at Lola's practically humping the air with her pelvis out and her arms back, followed by a moan.

"Ride my sailboat, BABY! Ask him if he has a big one," she said, winking. I couldn't help it; if anyone could make me laugh, it was Lola.

"LOLA!" I said in mock disbelief and slapped her shoulder. We burst out laughing as we made our way around the produce section, finishing up everything we needed, especially the bananas.

We headed towards the bread aisle, dancing to the music playing on the speakers, and I whipped out my phone.

"Sounds lovely. I would love to go for a ride. When is it good for you?" I wrote and hopped with excitement.

"I'm so happy for you! Maybe he has a single Dad for me? You know I like them old!" Lola said.

"You never know..." I picked up two loaves of bread and turned to Lola as I heard her talking to someone.

"Oh, what a small world! Konnichiwa!" she said happily.

"Konnichiwa! How nice to see you again, Lola!" the woman replied.

"What are you doing in Nantucket?"

"Just visiting family for the weekend," she smiled and pushed her son forward.

"Lola, this is my son, Hinata."

Lola bent down to shake his hand, a smile radiating on her face.

"Oh, hey, big guy. Nice to meet you. I am here with my best friend and her family. This is Ellie Edward. Ellie, this is Mika Fakumoto."

"So nice to meet you!" I said, extending my hand but stood awkwardly as she bowed forward instead. I didn't know what else to do, so I clumsily bowed as well. Great, now I look ridiculous!

"What a minute...Ellie Edward...Your name sounds familiar...Ellie Edward the same as Noelle Edward of The Edward Foundation?" she said, piecing it all together. It was always nice to know someone knew about it. I blushed and subconsciously pushed my shoulders back, appearing taller.

"Why, yes. You are familiar with my family's foundation?"

“Your family’s foundation has a special place in our heart. My mother was a single mother. We lost everything when we lost our father. She did her best, but when we fell on hard times, we had no place to go. She reached out to the foundation. I believe she met your father, John Edward, right? John?”

“She always said that he was her sweet angel. He helped us in our darkest days. It’s a true honor to meet you,” she said. I was so overwhelmed that I couldn’t hold back the tears. That truly was dad. Lola walked over to me and gently rubbed my back.

“It lovely to hear your story. Thank you for sharing it with me; it truly means a lot. It’s so amazing to hear such good things. All good things,” I said, my voice dripping with emotion.

“Can I give you a hug?” she asked, and I nodded happily. She smiled and took me into her embrace. I welcomed it completely. As soon as she moved away, I quickly wiped away my tears and looked at the little boy standing there, staring at us. I smiled at him, changing the subject.

“And you big man? You must be what, six years old?” I asked.

“No. I am seven years old,” he replied, offended, just as Eva would be.

“ANATA WA JIBUN JISHIN O FURUMAU," Mika said something to him that I didn't understand, but from the change in attitude, I could tell that she told him to behave himself.

“Sorry, but I am seven years old. Hi,” he said, looking embarrassed.

“Nice to meet you. My daughter is around here somewhere. She is seven as well. Her name is Eva.”

Just as I said it, I heard Eva’s shoes squeaking behind me as she ran up to us, giving me a big hug. I giggled as I looked down at her.

“We were just speaking about you, Love Bug,” I said. When I looked up, another Japanese man walked over and popped Hinata on his butt with a shopping cart. I have to admit, he looked quite dashing.

“Move it or lose it, Son,” he said, making Mika's cheeks turn red.

“Futoshi, this is Ellie Edward, my friend Lola from NYC, my single days...” she said, straining her voice as I often did with Lola when she was embarrassing me. The similarity was uncanny and also kind of cute.

“Nice to meet you, this is my daughter, Eva, and sister, Simone,” I introduced everyone. Just then, Futoshi leaned over and kissed my cheek, then did the same with Lola. As soon as he moved to Simone, Mika stepped forward to break up the lovefest. I could tell she was uncomfortable.

“So nice to meet you all. Sorry to rush off, but we must be going! We have to grab a few things and head to the boat. We can’t keep the Skipper waiting,” he said. I could still feel myself blushing as I smelled the Futoshi’s scent lingering on my cheek. I was so lost, I didn’t even realize that Futoshi was staring at me! I looked away quickly and quite uncomfortably.

“Ok, kids. It’s time to say goodbye," I said, and Eva stepped forward, surprising us all.

“Hajimemashite... Sayonara,” she said, bowing forward.

“Hajimemashite... Sayonara." Mika smiled and bowed. I was utterly dumbfounded. How did my seven-year-old know this stuff? I leaned into Lola and asked her, not hiding the amusement from my voice.

“My guess is YouTube Kids or Duolingo,” she said, making everyone laugh. We headed over to the cash register, and I glanced back to see the other three walking in the other direction.

“What a lovely family. How did you meet Mika?” I asked Lola.

“Partying at STK in the meatpacking district.”

“Our spot?" I asked in surprise, and she smiled.

“You know it, baby. She was knee-deep in daddy issues. I had to help a sister out,” she said, making me shake my head.

“I know. I know.”

“Mommy, what are daddy issues?" Eva's voice popped up, and I was so taken aback by the fact that she was hearing. Quickly, Simone jumped in with a smirk and put an arm around Eva, guiding her away. I kept myself close. I didn't want my sister telling Eva something she didn't need to know.

"Well, Eva, Daddy issues are… actually, you don't need to worry about Daddy issues until you are in your 20s. You have a very good Daddy who loves you very much. Your issues should be minimal," she said.

Eva looked down at her feet.

"I miss my daddy," she said. That was enough of that conversation. I quickly walked in between them and smiled at Eva.

"Hey, Love Bug, I know you miss your Dad. You will be with him in a few weeks and then during the week of Thanksgiving," I said excitedly, trying to get her excited as well.

"Oh, goodie, Mommy! But I will miss you guys." She looked at all of us.

"I know, Neecee. But you will be back with us before you know it," Simone said. We quickly moved through the checkout line, dancing with the music playing above. Eva was making faces, making us all laugh. We headed to the parking lot, loaded up the trunk, and hopped in the car.

"Cool plate. Doctor Money." Lola laughed, and I looked at the G500 with a Mass license plate that read 'DR ACK' parked in front of us. I laughed and turned on the ignition. The music immediately blasted through, making all of us dance and smile.

Chapter 10: Cooking Polish-y

When we reached home, we were all in a great mood. The blues slowly drifted away as we unpacked the groceries. Eva and Lola were busy talking while I was going through the items with Simone. Suddenly, I heard the familiar ding of my phone. I picked it up and saw it was a text from Jack.

"Hello, Noelle! The boys are available to start your roof tomorrow. We should be able to wrap it up this week," the text read.

"Sounds lovely. See you tomorrow!" I replied. I put my phone away and smiled excitedly.

"OK, girls! The new roof starts tomorrow! Let's discuss the game plan. Who's staying and who's going? Anyone takers for a Nantucket Christmas?" I said and laughed as Lola began doing her happy, sexy dance, moving her body with the rhythm of music supposedly playing in her head.

"I'm down! You know it... ho, ho, ho, hee, hee, hee!" I couldn't help it; I smiled even bigger.

"I'm not ready to go back to Maui. I miss Dad, and I feel his spirit around me here," she said, and I could sense the sadness in her voice. Suddenly, she perked up again and picked Eva up.

"It's beginning to look a lot like Christmas! I'm down!" she sang.

I was brimming with excitement, so much that tears of joy began to stream down my face.

"I love my girls! OK! Back to cooking! Who's got the hamburger?" I said.

"I've got the MEAT, baby!" Lola squealed in her ever so cheerful voice.

"I've got the Organic White Rice," Simone chipped in.

"Of course, you both do!" I said, laughing. I grabbed two large pots from the cupboard while Eva grabbed two cookie sheets and Simone grabbed three bowls. As per her usual self, Lola poured a glass of wine.

"Anyone want some? Oh... Yeah... What can I do to help?" she said as soon as she realized we were all getting busy with something or the other. I smiled at her.

"No, thank you. Just sit there and look pretty," I said.

"I will have some lemonade." Eva hopped up onto a seat.

"No, thanks," Simone said. Lola grabbed four glasses, poured Perrier water into three glasses, and kept one glass aside for lemonade. She handed them out, and Eva picked her glass.

"Cheers, everyone! I love you all very much!" she said, and I hugged her.

"Let the cooking commence!" I called out, and all the girls moved forward with their arms deep into the pile of food. I began to direct them on what to do while Simone began to place the cabbage in the pot of boiling water simmering on the stove. Lola poured rice into it while Eva broke eggs into a large bowl, her favorite thing to do.

"Mom, are six eggs enough?" she asked, looking up at me with her big, curious eyes.

"Plenty, darling, plenty," I called out. I looked up to see Lola walking over to her.

"We could make some OYAKODON with this mixture," she said.

"Oh, that sounds yummy, Lola. What's that?"

"It's Japanese cuisine. Of course, baby! I don't know how to make it, but I am sure we could take a trip to Japan and find out," she said, and I watched as Eva made yummy noises.

"I love dumplings too! Let's go, Lola!" she said excitedly.

"You are my little dumpling!" Lola tousled her hair. I could tell they were enjoying the cooking experience together, and I wanted to keep watching them.

"Let's scramble these little suckers!" Eva peered into the large bowl then picked it up with the meat mixture in it. As soon as she dumped the egg mixture in, I knew I had to go up and help her.

“That is perfect!” I said, looking in.

“PURRRRRRRRRRRRRRFECT! Right, Auntie?” Eva looked up at Simone.

“You got that right, girlfriend! PURRRRRRRRRRRRRRFECT!" She winked. It was such a calm, fun experience, and we all kept dancing our way around the kitchen.

We all joined Eva and put our hands into the bowl, picking up portions and making meatballs. We then gently placed them on different cookie sheets. Once we were done, I turned towards the stove and clapped my hands.

“Next up, the Chicken and Mushroom gravy!" I called out. Simone placed the meatballs in the oven, and Lola walked over to assist with the gravy. I picked up the whisk and felt Lola’s breath on my shoulder.

“My favorite part. Let me whip this gravy into shape,” she said, and I handed it to her.

“Here you go, Sweet Cheeks," I said. Simone and Eva were all over, first washing their hands and then dancing as they wiped them on the towel. My phone rang, and before I could reach it, Eva picked it up, her face glowing with happiness. Just looking at her, I knew it was her dad. Eva always had a special smile every time he called.

“Hi, Dad!” she squealed.

“Great, Dad! We are all cooking!” she answered after a while and walked towards me.

“All of you? Who’s all of you? Edward?" I could hear him say, and she giggled.

“No, Dad, don’t be silly. He is watching from the sofa. Mom, Lola, and Auntie.”

“Oh, I see. Everyone stayed. Interesting,” he said.

Edward was hunched over the sofa, and he stared at us in the kitchen.

“Yes, and they are staying through Christmas! Isn’t that great, dad?” she said excitedly, and I smiled at her.

“Sure, dad,” she said and handed me the phone.

“Dad wants to talk to you,” Eva said and ran over to Edward and pouted.

“Hello!” I said, stirring the pot.

“Hey, sorry we only had a few minutes at your Dad’s funeral to talk. I knew that wasn’t the place to discuss this but Thanksgiving plans? What would you like me to do this year?” he asked.

“Have you come up with any ideas yourself?” I asked, a little annoyed.

“I was thinking Aspen for some skiing or New York City for the parade, or both,” he said, and I felt my heart lift a little.

“She would love all of it!” I said and noticed Eva eavesdropping from the back.

“What, Mom? What would I love?” she asked.

“Darling, how does New York City for the Macy’s Day Parade and Aspen for some skiing sound?” I asked her.

“I used to love when you called me darling,” I heard Richard say, but I ignored it. Eva was now hopping up and down with excitement, and I cleared my throat.

“YES, MOM! YES!” she squealed.

"OK, Richard. Are you sure you don’t have to work?” I asked.

“Yes, I’m positive. I’ve rescheduled all my surgeries for the following week,” he said.

“OK, let me know when you’re going to pick her up and bring her back," I said and winked at Eva. She smiled. Eva loved her dad, and it felt so good to see her so excited.

“Sounds good,” Richard said softly.

“Excellent! We can talk about Christmas plans in December,” I said.

“Cool. Maybe a Christmas in Nantucket this year? One big happy family?” he said, and my voice went flat, immediately bringing the girls' attention to me.

“Probably not. Goodbye, Richard,” I said.

“Bye, Dickie!” Lola called out.

"Bye-Bye, Richie!" Simone said.

"Goodbye, Noelle. Goodbye, girls!" Richard said, almost sounding amused as I cut the call. The girls all burst out laughing. As the silence faded, Eva's tiny voice grabbed all of our attention.

"Mom, I miss Dad," she said. I bent to her and smiled at her.

"I know, honey bear. It's OK. We both love you very much!" I said, hugging her.

We quickly went back to cooking until the sweet aroma of food began to rise. Quickly, we proceeded to put down the delicious food on the table and could not control the hunger pangs anymore. It all smelled and looked so good! We sat down in front of it, and before starting, Simone smiled at me.

"I would like to say a prayer in Dad's honor," she said.

"Sounds lovely." I smiled at her. She closed her eyes and bowed her head.

"We receive this food in gratitude to all beings. We thank all those who have helped to bring it to our table. We honor and preserve our Polish values..." she said, and Eva knew that once Simone began, she wouldn't stop.

"Amen. Can we eat now?" she said eagerly.

Simone laughed. "Dig in, everyone!" she said, and immediately, the sound of cutlery went around. Everyone dug in as though they had been hungry for the longest time. No doubt, it all tasted amazing!

"So, Mom. Can we have a Halloween Party?" Eva asked, looking at me with her puppy dog eyes again. She knew I could never say no to that.

"Umm... how about yes!" I said.

"Puuuuurrrfect!" Simone laughed.

"I have a great idea! It could be Japanese themed." Lola chimed in.

"I love it! We can serve dumplings!" Eva said excitedly.

"Or we could do a Hawaiian theme," Simone said.

"I love that idea too! Hawaiian Pizza for everyone!"

"Eva, what are your thoughts?" I asked Eva.

"Well, I was really thinking it could be a Day of the Dead Party!" she said, taking me by surprise.

"We can celebrate Gramps!" she said. I was not expecting that. It immediately brought a pang of sadness and my eyes brimmed with tears. Simone choked up too, and Lola cleared her throat.

"I love it!" Simone smiled.

"I'm down! Let's plan a fiesta!"

"Eva, you are the sweetest girl I know. Day of the Dead it is!" I said happily.

Chapter 11: The Roof is on Fire

I was at the kitchen counter, sipping some coffee when I heard a couple of trucks pulling into the driveway. I was going to get up, but I saw Simone closer to the door in her yoga outfit. I was too busy taking in the quiet, bright morning to actually move from my spot. I looked at the watch on my wrist.

9 AM. Right on time, impressive.

A few moments later, there was a knock on the door, and Simone walked over to open it.

"You must be the roofer. Nice crew!" I heard her say. Outside, there were footsteps of guys unloading the roofing supplies on the side of the house. Edward was barking in one of the rooms, trying to get out to Jack.

"Yes. Hi, I'm Andrew Jackson, but my friends call me Jack."

"Nice to meet you. I'm Simone," she said, and I smiled at the very obvious flirting in her voice.

"Is Noelle home?" Jack asked.

"Yes. Come on in. She's in the kitchen."

Right then, I saw Jack pop his head in and smile.

"Oh, good morning, Jack. How's the arm?" I put the mug down and greeted him. He shrugged and looked at the cast.

"The doctor said one more week and then back to normal."

"Normal?" I giggled. Jack gave me a stern look; if anything, he looked even sexier.

"Yes! Normal. Wise Ass," he said, and I burst out laughing with him. Simone rolled her eyes and smiled as she walked in. As if noticing her for the first time, Jack became serious again and got on track.

"So... I've got the guys setting up outside. If you need anything, give me a shout. They should be wrapping it up by Friday," he said, just as I stood to take out the leftovers from last night's dinner from the refrigerator.

"That looks delicious!" he said, perking up. His eyes never leaving the bowl. Before I could say anything, Simone jumped in.

"Are you hungry, Jack? Let me make you something. Do you like Polish meatballs?" she asked as Jack hungrily ogled at the food.

"Sound amazing!" he said hungrily. The light footsteps entered the kitchen, and I saw Lola standing at the entrance in a bright red kimono. As soon as she saw Jack, her eyes lit up.

"GOOD MORNING!" she greeted excitedly. I smiled at her to calm herself.

"Good Morning! This is Jack, the roofer. Jack, this is Lola." I said and then shook my head as I saw Lola checking Jack out head to toe.

"So nice to meet you, Jack," she said as she swirled around him like a buzzing bee and touched his arm. Jack watched her, then quickly switched his attention back to Simone. He looked like he was trapped in a den of lionesses, and it was almost amusing to watch!

"I'll have a few," he told Simone.

"Would you like some rye bread and butter?" Simone asked, and his smile grew even more if that was possible.

"Sure. Outstanding. I need to come over here more often." He laughed. I noticed Lola standing there, never moving her eyes from Jack. It was evident that she was noting his every move.

"Our door is always open, Jack," she said. I walked up to them and perched myself up onto one of the seats.

"Yes, it's always the Royal treatment with these two around." I giggled.

"I'm heading up to take a cold shower," Lola announced and walked out of the kitchen, which had suddenly filled with the amazing aroma of food.

"Here you go, Jack." Simone handed him a plate, and he took it graciously. I could almost see the drool on the side of his mouth.

"Thank you, Simone."

"OK, Sissy, I'm heading out for my 10 AM Yoga class," Simone looked over at me and gave me a suggestive smile before leaving the room. Jack sat up and puffed out his chest. It was hard to miss his manly stature. He made it too obvious to miss.

"So, Noelle, I was thinking..." he began, and I smiled as I leaned in.

"Yes, Jack, what were you thinking?" I looked straight into his eyes, already knowing what he was about to say.

"I would like to take you out to dinner," he finally said, and I could feel my heart leap from my chest. It was odd but nice.

"Oh yes, you do owe me. Is Mr. Pickles picking up the check?"

"Of course, he is! How about Friday?" he asked.

"Let me check my schedule," I said. I watched as his plate slowly emptied away. It was now his turn to look me straight in my eyes.

"We should be wrapping up the roof by then, and Mr. Pickles would be so upset if you did not accept his apology," he said, and I smiled.

"OK. Sure. I accept," I said slowly, pretending to think. He had a pleased smile on his face, and then he stood up to leave the house.

"See you Friday at Jackson's. How about 7?" he asked as he stood by the door.

"Sounds perfect!" I said, but I couldn't help but be a little concerned. The moment he left, I rushed over to the office and sat down on my large blue desk. As soon as I turned on the computer, Lola popped into the office.

"So you have a date Friday night with Mr. Senior Sexy? I have to be honest, he's more my type," she said, waltzing over to me.

"I know; I know, but Mr. Pickles owes me." We both laughed, just as my phone rang. I picked it up to see Drew's name on the screen.

"Weather looks good for Friday. Does 11 AM work for you?" he had texted. I smiled.

"Who's that?" Lola leaned in, trying to look into my screen.

"Drew. He wants a sailing date on Friday at 11 AM."

"So... Two dates on Friday! You go, girl! PLAYA!" she said and hooted. I rolled my eyes.

"Oh, yeah, Playa."

"Sounds lovely," I typed.

"Friday's going to be busy," Lola said.

"Yes, I guess so. Good thing Richard's coming for Eva."

"Cool! I'm going for a run to town for a latte. Do you want anything?" she said, turning around. I leaned back in my chair.

"No thanks, Bestie!" I called out to her. As she left the house, I made a few updates on the invite list and finished the invitation for the Edward Foundation Annual Gala, then hit send. I felt overwhelmed yet accomplished a good combination!

My eyes went to the bookcase in front of me and the photo framed lined up. I stood up, stretched, and walked over to them to see the pictures there. Memories of dad came flooding in, taking me back to the good old days.

It physically hurt me, and there was nothing I could take to ease the pain. As my vision blurred with my tears, I picked up a photo and ran my fingers through dad's image of him smiling with me at a Patriots game.

"Done, Dad! This is going to be the best fundraiser yet! You would be so proud of me!" I whispered, smiling. After a while, I placed the photo back on the shelf and wiped away the tears. I had to put my brave face on again.

Chapter 12: The Harbor Date

I held my phone in front of my face as I stared at his text for a moment.

"Can't wait to see you tomorrow, Gorgeous."

I couldn't help but smile as I read this text from Drew. I didn't reply. Instead, I put my phone back on the nightstand and slumbered into a blissful sleep.

As the sunlight hit my eyes, I opened them to see the soft swishing of the curtains. Finally, it was Friday, the day of my two dates. I laid in bed, feeling completely and utterly relaxed for a moment. I felt my mind free of all the worries and concerns of the world. I couldn't believe that I was excited!

I chuckled at the thought of the two dates I had today with two men that were poles apart from each other. I knew it was unlike me to do something like this, but that didn't mean I couldn't do it.

Eva was in school, and I didn't check to see if Lola and Simone were home. I was still in my bed, thinking about both the guys as my eyes naively fell upon the tiny clock on my nightstand. I leaped out of my bed as the clock read 9:55 am.

Did I just waste 50 minutes in all that daydreaming?! I rushed towards the bathroom and tried my best to look a little more presentable.

I shrugged out of jammies and slipped on the outfit that I had carefully picked out for my date. It was perfect, but not too fancy, but it was cute enough to make me feel confident.

I had chosen out a jumpsuit, with its color bright enough to flatter me in the bright, shining sun at sea. I swiftly wore the outfit and completed my outfit with a pair of Sperry's and a small Chanel cross-body bag. I looked at my reflection one last time in the mirror. Pleased with the result, I added a quick touch of gloss on my lips and snuck out the door to meet Drew at the Nantucket Boat Basin.

I carefully parked my car and checked the time, relieved to see that I was only five minutes late. I got out of my SUV in an attempt to look for Drew when my eyes landed on all the yachts that were lined up. They stretched out till the end of the dock. I could see the sailboats and boats as far as my eyesight allowed me to look. Everything was postcard perfect.

It was a beautiful, windy morning. The sun was peeking through the clouds, and the rays were gentle enough not to cause any sunburn. It was good because, in all the hurry, I had forgotten to wear sunscreen. I scanned the parking lot for signs of Drew when I noticed his car parked nearby. There I saw him getting out of his Range Rover. He saw me and flashed his charming smile, then quickly walked over to me with a basket in his hands.

As Drew walked the last step towards me, he leaned forward and kissed me on the cheek as I sensed his sunglasses fall off his head. I blushed a little as I heard him say.

"Whoops. I can be so clumsy at times. Damn you, Drew," He said, getting a little self-conscious.

Drew and I both leaned forward at the same time to pick his sunglasses off the ground. Then our heads knocked together like coconuts. Drew looked up at me, putting his hand on his head, acting as I had injured him. I laughed along with him. It was like an instant connection. Somewhere, I could hear Lola making some joke about it.

"So nice to see you, Gorgeous." He said with the cutest little smile on his face.

"So nice to see you, Darlin- I mean Drew," I responded as the flush in my cheeks deepened. Boy, what a great time for a slip of the tongue!

"I like that." He smiled.

"Oh, I packed us a little picnic! I hope you like what I've selected," He laughed heartily, clearly enjoying himself as he pointed towards the basket in his hand.

"Sounds perfect. You are so thoughtful." I replied. Wow! He did put a lot of thought and effort into it. I could work with this.

"Well, I hope so. My mother raised me right. So, hopefully, you like fruit, cookies with a side of cheese, and a little lobster Caprese salad to top it off. Oh, and we can't forget the freshly brewed tea." Drew studied my face for any reaction. I could feel saliva fill my mouth, and my eyes lit up with excitement.

"Delicious! It's everything I love," I couldn't contain the delight in my voice. He had not only managed to arrange this flawlessly romantic date but also brought the perfect food.

Drew smiled at me as we walked down to sailboat slip. I could hear the seagulls as they soared above me. He asked me to wait while he was busy loading the medium size sailboat with the basket and blankets. I didn't mind; I liked watching him. He reappeared after a while and held his hand out to assist me in the boat.

If I hadn't said it before, he was quite the gentleman. We slipped into each other's arms as soon as I set foot inside the yacht. I felt this strong magnetic attraction between us. It was so rare; I knew something magical was happening. This date was so much better than anything I would have imagined.

Drew held his eyes on me as if he was studying every feature of my face. He stopped at my eyes and looked deep into them. Then, suddenly, I sensed his warm lips on top of mine as we submerged into a kiss. Electricity bolted through my body as I felt him against me.

“I couldn’t resist your lips, Gorgeous.” He said shyly as he caressed my face. His tone may be shy, but there was nothing about that kiss that looked nervous to me. It made me feel sexy and empowered.

“Drew, Darling, please don’t stop with those sweet lips and sweet words,” I said as my senses focused on his lips.

“Ok, Gorgeous. I think I can manage that!” He laughed, his face filled with content.

I looked at him, smiling enticingly. I just couldn't help myself. He leaned into me slowly again, and his lips landed on mine. The urgency was ecstatic, and we kissed until the boat began to rock a little. Drew then pulled away, leaving a feeling of emptiness on my lips.

“As much as I hate this to end, we need to sit down and get the boat moving out of the harbor. Safety first.” He said.

“Aye, Aye, Captain Drew, Darling,” I pouted as I saw him move away from me. However, I continued to look in his direction like an attentive puppy.

As I studied Drew, I put my hand over my mouth and snapped out of the scenery of this utterly romantic date. Suddenly, I found myself thinking about my date later tonight with Jack.

“Enjoy this. Stay in the moment. Men do this all the time,” I murmured to myself when I heard the engine start again.

“What is that, Ellie? Sorry, I couldn’t hear you.” Drew called out, his voice muffled under all the noise from the engine.

“Oh, I was asking if there was anything I can do to help?” I responded, trying to sound as casual as I could.

“You’re doing it, Gorgeous.” I felt myself glowing as he complimented me once again. I took a deep breath and succeeded in putting Jack out of my mind.

Drew started motoring out of the boat basin towards the open harbor and then passed the lighthouse. As I looked out at the calm sea ahead of us and I couldn’t help but think of my dad.

“My father used to sail me around the island when I was a child,” I said as I reminisced about the good old days. Even on a perfect day like today, I couldn’t help but think about dad.

"My dad did, as well. I loved it." He replied in his sweet, comforting voice.

We both smiled at one another, and slowly, he leaned over. I felt him get closer, and then he kissed me again, and again, and again, and again. Everything else began to fade away in the background. It was as if we were the only two people in the world. All I felt was the soft drifting of the boat, but I couldn’t tell if it was the rush of emotions or just the boat.

All of a sudden, I felt a drop of water on my cheek. I assumed it was the water splash from the sea, so I didn't really pay attention to it. We were so engrossed in each other that we carried on kissing, but the drops continued to multiply. Finally, when it was too much, we both stopped kissing to take a look. Much to our surprise, we opened our eyes only to notice a big rain cloud coming. My mouth dropped open, the intensity of the kiss fading away.

"Oh, Drew! Look at that!" I pointed to the raging cloud making its way to us, my voice filled with concern.

"The weather report said nothing about showers!" Drew said as he looked at his cell phone.

"Oh, man! I had it set on Boston weather!" Drew went on as the rain began to pour down. Suddenly, everything was a rush as we scrambled through the sailboat, trying not to get soaked.

Drew stood up and stretched his hand as he signaled me to hold it. I did and followed him as he led me towards the cabin.

"You will be safe down here. I need to take the sails down. I will be right back." Drew said as he ran back up to the sails. I felt the boat rocking back and forth and up and down and began to feel nauseous. Suddenly, I saw Drew get sideswiped by the sails and fall, and the loud thump followed.

"ARE YOU OK, DREW?" I yelled so he could hear me.

There was no response, so I stood up and called out again, louder this time.

"ARE YOU OK?" Just then, I saw Drew from there, drenching in the rain and looking like he needed help. I tried making my way over to him when he stopped me.

"YES, I WILL BE DOWN IN A MINUTE! GO BACK IN! DO NOT COME HERE," He instructed me, and I ducked back into safety.

The cabin may have seemed like a blessing, but really, I could feel myself starting to sweat and get dizzy again. I saw a can of iced tea in the room, so I grabbed it and began sipping it in hopes that this would calm my nausea. However, it didn't help much. It only made everything worse because, as soon as I stopped sipping, I heard my stomach make a growling noise, and I immediately threw up all over the cabin floor.

This was not my idea of an ideal date!

I side-eyed Drew as he entered the cabin.

Great! What a perfect time to make an entry! However, Drew, being Drew, didn't say anything and stepped close to me. He grabbed a bucket from the corner and held my hair back, slowly rubbing my back to make me feel better.

"I'm so sorry, Drew. This never happens." I said, trying to hide my face away from him. I wanted to look cute, and here I was throwing up! There was nothing cute about that.

"It's OK, Gorgeous. Don't worry you pretty little head. I am here for you." Drew replied understandingly. I admired his kindness. He was so much more than just a pretty face.

The boat's rocking slowed down and, slowly, I began to feel better too. I had been on the sea many times, and this had never happened to me. Maybe I was nauseous because of the thought of my other date tonight, or perhaps it really was the sea.

Drew held me closer to his chest, his affection comforting me. I was snuggled deep in his chest when I heard my cell phone ding in, and when I saw the screen, it was a text from Lola. Drew's face was just above mine, placed perfectly for him to read it over my shoulder.

"A storm is coming! Be careful! How's the date going with Mr. Sexy?" The text read. I looked back at him, and the two of us burst out laughing.

"He's great, and I just threw up," I responded with a green-faced emoji giving away too much information.

My phone dinged back almost immediately.

"BAHAHAHAHAHAHAHAHA! ELLIE, Classic!"

Well, at least someone was having a good laugh out of my misery. I put my phone away, shaking my head.

Drew got up and grabbed me a hand towel. He then went somewhere and came back with a wet face cloth and handed it to me. I quickly grabbed it and cleaned myself up. Relieved that there would be no possibility of throw up chunks stuck to my face.

“Can I get you anything?” Drew asked as he cleaned up the vomit from the floor with some Windex.

“Do you have any crackers?” I ask him innocently. I watched as he walked towards a little cupboard, grabbed a box of oyster crackers, and handed me a few.

“Thank you, Darling,” I said as I nibbled on a few. He then proceeded to offer some more crackers to me, then embraced me in a hug. He pulled me closer to him as he continued to cuddle and comfort me in his arms.

“Once this passes, I will get you back to shore.” He whispered.

"I don't want this to end," I replied. I was being honest. Drew was nothing short of perfect, and this was the most beautiful date I had been on if we didn't include the fact that I threw up in front of him.

We gazed into each other's eyes, and then Drew kissed my forehead.

“Me neither, Gorgeous. Me neither.” I heard him say as we kissed one more time.

Chapter 13: Girl Time

As I headed back home after my wonderful date, I couldn't shake the feeling of how incredible I felt when I was with Drew. I was on cloud 9!

He was more than perfect, more than what I had originally thought of. Everything that happened created a whole new memory I didn't want to let go of.

With thoughts of my date with Drew running across my mind, I came inside my bedroom and stripped down, throwing my clothes in the hamper. I headed to the bathroom and hopped in the hot shower as I chewed down some tums.

My thoughts didn't help me much in making a decision, but they did bring me back the fresh memory of today's date. I mean, it's not my fault because I had a brilliant day today, all thanks to Drew. We had a connection and, I suddenly didn't know if I should go out with Jack and put myself in a position of doubt.

Drew was way more my type than Jack, right? I was clearly in a spiral as I contemplated going out with Jack tonight.

I was debating with myself when I heard a voice that snapped me back to reality.

"HEY! SO what happened with Mr. Foxy Kitten?" Lola asked.

“SHIT! You scared me!” I almost screamed, unaware that someone was here with me in the bathroom. I saw Lola sitting on the bathroom stool, and my reaction sent her into a fit of laughter.

"Sorry, I couldn't wait! Tell me! Tell me!" Lola said as her eyes plead for more information. She puts her feet up on the bathtub, fully aware that this was a bathroom, not a locker room.

"Well…we were kissing, and a storm crept upon us, and then, basically, I threw up," I answered her question with as little information as possible. She smirked at me.

“So, is he a good kisser?” Lola asked. Even more interested in my answer than she was in the previous one.

“UMMMMM YES! But then the storm stopped us,” I replied with a smile building on my lips just at the thought of Drew.

“Ohhhhhh, darn New England weather! Always creeping in!”

“He was so sweet while I was barfing in the cabin. He held my hair back.”

“OHHHHHHHHHHHHHHH! How sweet!” Lola said as she made puppy eyes. Lola always had been like this – too invested in my life.

“Kind of disgusting,” I responded as I reenacted my puking performance. Throwing up on a date is everything but sweet.

"You are crazy! That is the sweetest thing I ever heard. He must like you a lot, or he wants your sweet stuff!” Lola said as she winked at me.

"LOLA!" I replied, faking a horrified expression. To be fair, I should've seen this coming. After all, Lola does say whatever comes to her mind.

"Well! I'm just honest!" Lola laughed, putting her arms in the air implying that she meant no harm.

"You're right about one part, though; he was very sweet and charming! He asked me out for dinner on Sunday night." I said. I could sense myself blushing. However, more than me, my answer made Lola squeal with joy.

"OHHHH, GIRL! OHHHHHHHHHHHHHHH GIRL!" She sounds happier than I was. Actually, no. I was a lot chirpier; I just was trying to contain it.

“I know, I know!” I replied, trying to contain my excitement.

“So what about tonight? Are you still going?” Lola asked. Her face was filled with amusement – she was asking the hard questions now.

"Of course, I'm still going. Mr. Pickles owes me a dinner," I replied as we both laughed. Well, now that I've told her I'm going, I have to fulfill my commitment.

“Hand me a towel, Chickadee!” I said as I stepped out of the shower.

“You got it, Sex Queen!’ Lola said cheekily as she hits me in the butt. We both started laughing again.

“What should I wear for my dinner date? Casual or Fancy? "I asked, looking at Lola. She always gave excellent advice, so it only made sense to ask her for outfit recommendations too.

“Girl! You never go casual,” Lola said as she looked at me as if I was insane for asking that question.

“I know, I know.” I nodded approvingly.

"Oh, I forgot to tell you, Simone and Eva were heading out for a yoga class, and when she was done, she is going to drop her off with Richard at the ferry," Lola got up from the floor, and I watched her as she makes her way out the door.

“Oh, she will love that!” I replied.

“They both looked pretty excited. I told them to go get some Zen for me,” I heard Lola’s voice from a distance. She was well in the other room by this time.

I made my way out of the bathroom as I closed the door behind me and went to my closet to pick out a fancy cocktail dress to wear. I felt like dressing up, not to impress Jack, just for myself. I wore the most excellent dress I could find, and I walked out of my room to show my dress to Lola.

When I stepped out, Lola's jaw dropped wide enough for Edward to fit his face in. She looked at me top to bottom and then bottom to top again, shaking her head like she had lost her mind. She was exaggerating.

“Lola, you are so funny!” I said as I looked at Lola’s expression.

“LOOK AT YOU, SEX QUEEN! You are going to excite that old man! He won’t even need the V nugget!” Lola says cheekily.

I put my hands on my eyes in embarrassment. Lola does say whatever she wants whenever she wants.

“Hmmm, maybe I should change and put on my sweatpants,” I say as I put my finger on my chin in an attempt to think.

“That old man would get even more excited! A girl in sweatpants is every man’s dream!” Lola said as she was having too much fun embarrassing me.

"Stop, Lola. You're making me nervous," I said as I shake my head and burst out laughing. 'God, this girl never stops, does she?' I thought to myself as I finished getting ready for my second date of the day.

Chapter 14: Friday Date Round 2

As I pulled into the driveway of this incredibly fancy restaurant, I read the name glowing in flashing lights, "JACKSON'S." I've always wanted to go there. It's a seamless combination of fancy but casual, perfect for a first date.

"Jackson's made it on time," I said to myself as I looked at my watch.

I walk into the restaurant, overwhelmed by the smell of roses. I noticed that the restaurant is dark and romantically lit with candles on every table.

As I peered into the restaurant, searching for Jack, I felt a gentle tap on my shoulder. I turned around only to be greeted by Jack and his dazzling toothy smile. I glanced over at him to see what he's wearing for the date, subtle enough for him not to take notice that I was checking him out.

He's wearing dark washed fitted-jeans, a baby blue button-up shirt with just enough buttons undone to make me curious, and a chic brown sports coat.

If his outfit could talk, it would say, "I'm serious about this and you." And damn it, he looked good. WAY TOO GOOD!

"Hey, you! I was just looking for you." I coolly said as I tried to control my urge to gawk at him.

"Can I take your coat?" Jack asked as he came and stood beside me to hold my coat.

"Such a gentleman. Of course," I responded.

As I was in the process of taking off my coat. Jack leaned in and kissed my cheek. I was taken aback and felt a little awkward since I did not expect it. In what world do you not give a girl warning before you do that?

"Good Evening, let me show you to your table, Mr. Jackson." The waiter interrupted us. The name tag on his tag read "Sebastian."

"Thank you, Sebastian," Jack said to him politely.

As we walked toward our table, Jack reached out to pull out a chair for me to sit down. Our chairs faced each other, and I was glad the table was between us.

"Here are the menus. Andrea will be over shortly to share the evening specials." Sebastian said as he handed us our abnormally tall menus.

"Thank you," Jack replied gently.

"Thank you," I said to Sebastian, too, as he began to leave.

I was going in over my head about things to talk to him when he leaned in once more. Oh god, I really hope he doesn't take me by surprise; that would be twice in the first ten minutes of our date.

"You look ravishing," Jack said as he looked into my eyes.

Thank God he didn't kiss me on my cheek again. I just wasn't ready for it this soon.

"Thank you, Jack, you clean up nicely yourself," I said as a smile formed on my lips. Well, I was telling the truth. He did look nice, and I was no liar.

"Do you like wine?" He said as he pointed to the drink menu.

"Yes, but only a little," I responded. I was in no mood to get drunk today. I wanted to behave and hopefully not do anything I would regret later on.

"What type do you prefer?" Jack asked me, his face now even closer than it was before. It was like he didn't care that it was a restaurant.

"Red, please," I responded, leaning back slightly. I didn't want him to think I was uncomfortable, but I was really trying to conduct myself better.

"OK, my favorite. Do you prefer Californian or Italian?" Jack said. I didn't know if he just had this habit of agreeing with everyone or was I just special.

"Either," I responded safely.

I did come to the date, but I was in no mood of giving Jack any signals. As we talked about nothing, I noticed the waitress walking toward us.

'Hello, Mr. Jackson." She said.

Interesting! The waitress knew him, and it certainly piqued my interest.

"Andrea, so nice to see you," Jack said as he stood up and gave her a kiss on her cheek.

Is this Jack's thing? Why does he keep kissing people on the cheek? Seeing this exchange between these two, I certainly didn't feel as weird as I did before?

"Always a pleasure. Would you like a bottle of the usual?" She asked Jack with a soft smile.

"Yes, please," Jack responded with an even softer smile taking over his face.

"Miss, what would you like to dri-?" She said as she turned her head toward me. But before she could finish, Jack interrupted her mid-sentence.

"Oh, Andrea, you are funny. We will be sharing." Jack said as he started laughing.

The waitress looked at me and winked as he said that, but I couldn't help and feel that her stare was a little serious. I didn't know what to make of it.

"May I share with you the specials?" The waitress asked us as she was now looking at Jack. We both nod our heads in consent.

"Yes, please," Jack said. His voice was filled with enthusiasm.

"Chef has prepared a lovely Veal Marsala with roasted potatoes and mixed vegetable medley. Secondly, butternut squash ravioli smothered in an Alfredo sauce. Lastly, a nice piece of red snapper in a spicy red tomato sauce with a side of broccoli." The waitress said to us as she read out the specials from the day.

And then she took a step back, not leaving us but getting far enough to give us the privacy to decide.

"Sounds amazing!' I responded as I looked in her direction.

"The Veal Marsala is the best!" Jack said to me.

"Have you decided?" The waitress returned quicker than I had anticipated, but it was good for me because I already knew what I wanted to eat.

"My favorite dish! The Veal Marsala, please," I said as my mouth filled with water. I couldn't wait to eat, I was hungry, and I might as well get a good meal out of this date.

"I just had the veal the other day. I will have the Chef's Ravioli." Jack answered, taking a look at the menu one more time before he handed her the menu.

"Excellent choice. I will put that in and grab your bottle of wine, Mr. Jackson." She said.

As the waitress finally left our table and made her way toward the kitchen. I could feel Jack staring at me when he asked, "So, how was your day?"

I wanted to spare him from the details because, if I was completely honest, my day was much better than my night. So, I just stuck to the basics.

"A little rough but turned out to be a great day," I responded with as little details as I could do away with.

Jack laughed as he heard me respond.

"Just a little rough? That little squall that came through earlier was like a mini hurricane." He said as he reminded me of my boat adventures, which eventually led to the unfortunate throwing up incident on the boat.

I could not help but laugh as I remembered the complete idiot I had made of myself earlier today.

"You can say that again. We didn't see it coming, and then it just hit! Crazy weather," I responded.

"That's New England for you," Jack said, looking over the open sky staring right at us. Maybe, he was making sure the weather would not pull anymore dirty tricks tonight.

"Yes. I completely agree." I answered. He was right. I mean, out of all the days, the stupid mini hurricane had to come today. But at least Drew and I got a great story out of it. As I was engulfed in my thoughts about Drew and my morning with him, I sensed the waitress almost sneaking upon us with a bottle of what looked like an expensive bottle of wine.

As soon as she reached our table, she opened it and poured it first into Jack's glass. I was a little surprised when I noticed her fill his glass entirely from top to bottom.

"Bellissimo! Always Perfecto!" Jack said as he took a big sip of the wine.

The waitress then turned toward me and poured me almost half a glass, which is perfect. There is absolutely no need for me to drink a lot tonight.

"Thank you, very nice. Tastes exquisite." I said to the waitress as I sipped a little bit of my drink. It really was great!

"Exquisite is what I was going for," Jack said, staring into my eyes. I broke the gaze and looked in another direction. I really wished this restaurant was not as romantic as it was.

Jack had already drunk half of his glass by the time I had only managed to drink one sip.

As I was about to take my second sip, Jack leaned forward toward me. It made me aware of his profound gaze.

"So... I finally have you all to myself." He said.

I was about to respond when I heard my cell phone ring—saved by the bell, quite literally! As I look toward my phone's screen, I saw a text message from none other than Mr. Sexy, AKA Drew.

I could not help but smile. There was just something about him that made me feel like a teenage girl in high school. I knew I had to excuse myself if I wanted to look normal, and that is what I exactly did.

"Excuse me, I need to take this. It's my daughter." I lied. I couldn't be honest. I couldn't really tell him, "Hey, it's a message from the guy I saw before coming here." Yeah, nope, that was not the right way to go.

"Sure. Sure. Go ahead." Jack responded. It was evident that he was frustrated by the frequent people that had interrupted our 'date.'

As I stood from my chair to head toward the bathroom, I saw Jack grab a pill from his jacket pocket and pop it in his mouth. He then swigged it down with a mouth full of wine. I thought I'd be the weird one today, but I guess not!

I could not wait to reach the bathroom to read the message. So, I open my phone in the middle and read the message that Drew had sent me on my short stroll toward the bathroom.

TEXT MESSAGE: Hi Gorgeous! I hope you are feeling better.

I smiled as I looked at my phone. I must have looked like some idiot because I noticed our waitress from tonight look at me with the weirdest expression on her face. Haha! But she did not know why I was smiling, so I was safe.

As I was thinking of what to respond to Drew's text, I went inside the bathroom stall and put down the toilet seat. I sat on it like it was my living room chair.

TEXT MESSAGE: Drew Darling, you are so sweet. Thank you, I am feeling much better.

My phone buzzed again, and if it was capable of showing emotions, it would be smiling as big as me.

TEXT MESSAGE: Excellent! Looking forward to Sunday night already!

I take no more than a second to respond. After all, it's Drew that we're talking about here.

TEXT MESSAGE: Me too! I'm heading to bed now.

I couldn't help but feel a little guilty about lying. There was literally no point in lying; I could have just told him I was out. I really have to start thinking before I text.

TEXT MESSAGE: Good idea, get some rest. Good Night Gorgeous.

As I came back to my seat, I looked at Jack's glass. He was already on his second fill of wine. He really was fast at gulping down those drinks. When I was seated back in my seat, the waitress arrived with bread and butter.

"Is everything ok? So, where were we?"

Jack asked me a pompous question. I knew he wasn't really interested in knowing what happened. He only wanted to get back to making googly eyes at me. I could sense he was getting a little fidgety because he quickly sipped down another glass of wine and stretched out his neck to look for the waitress. When he caught her eye, he tapped the empty bottle, signaling for the second bottle of wine.

"Everything is fine," I answered. I was no longer interested in the conversation, but I was still quite curious about his behavior.

"Oh, good. So, Noelle, what do your weekends usually look like?" Jack asked another question.

"Spending time with my daughter, sometimes catching a movie, fun stuff like that," I answered.

Well, not this Sunday, though! I thought in my head as a playful smile crept on my lips.

"Oh, I was hoping you'd be available tomorrow night for Round 2," Jack said.

I laughed at his invitation. He had got to be kidding me.

"Oh, you're serious?" I asked, my eyes almost coming out of my head.

Did he really think our night was going well enough for me to want to do this again?

Jack took another big gulp from his glass as I sipped my drink nervously. As he drank, his eyes stayed glued to me. He didn't bother to untie his gaze.

I was starting to get uncomfortable, and I wanted to change the subject. As my mind ran wild with the least romantic questions, I stopped on one.

"So, Jack, what was the last book you really got into?" I asked, hoping my question would divert his attention. Jack's reaction to my question was delayed, but he quickly snapped out of whatever zone he was in.

"I don't read," he responded plainly.

"Oh, ok. Favorite movies?" I asked again.

Give me a little something to work with here, Jack. I can't continue the conversation if you don't help me out here.

"Hmmm....Let's see, the last movie that I really like was The Departed. OG movies are my favorite. That's my style." He responded this time as he actually thought about it.

But I couldn't help and notice that his tone was getting a little weirder. If I didn't know him, I would say it was almost as if he was talking to me rudely. But I shrugged it off.

"Oh, I see. I don't think I saw that one." I said as I looked at him.

Just when we had found the least romantic topic to talk about, the waitress came with our dinner and Jack's much-awaited second bottle of wine.

"Here we go!" She said as she handed Jack the bottle.

"Looks fantastic," Jack responded as he quickly took the bottle away from her.

"Great," I said as I looked at all the food.

Everything looked incredibly delicious. The date was awkward, but the food was enough to cheer me up.

"You are beautiful," Jack said as he started to stare at me again. His stare wasn't romantic at all. It was irritating.

"I will have a glass of Perrier with a lime," I said to the waitress as I ignored Jack's stare.

"I will get that right away." The waitress responded as she moved away from our table.

I did not want to be rude, so I knew I had to thank him for the compliment, or else, who knows how many bottles of wine this man would gulp if I didn't acknowledge his praises.

"Thank you, Jack. " I responded in the politest way I could.

I could not wait to get over with this dinner. I wasn't going to waste another second listening to another boring conversation about literally nothing in particular.

As I dug into my food with my intention to finish it off quickly, I looked at Jack's plate, who was eating twice as slow as he drank since all I see him do was pouring down the wine.

"So, Noelle, what is the most adventurous thing you've done?" Jack asked me. He actually looked interested.

He winked at me, entirely misreading the situation, which only made me a little more pissed than I was earlier. This night was turning out to be a mistake. I should have canceled when I had the chance.

"Let's see, most adventurous. Hmmmmmm..." I took my time to respond.

Jack looked eager, so eager that he stopped eating, put his fork down, and grabbed his wine again. His obsession with his wine was starting to piss me off. I felt a little more awkward with every passing second.

"Jack, I would have to say traveling to Mumbai by myself," I said as I finally decided on the answer.

"Mumbai... India?" Jack said with shock in his voice.

"Oh, yes, it was amazing. The foods, people, culture. On my way home, I traveled to Nepal and picked up some Buddhist prayer flags for my father." I said. I remembered all of it like it was yesterday. It was a great memory.

"India? Why would you want to go to that place?" Jack inquired, almost as if he was mad at my answer.

"I always wanted to expose myself to the rich colors of the country. I have a passion for fabrics." I responded as I was slightly offended by his tone of questioning.

This conversation was leading nowhere.

"The colors of the country?" He asked.

Ugh. Yet another senseless question...precisely like this date.

"So, Jack, what is the most adventurous thing you've ever done?" I asked as I didn't want to answer his question. Jack took another big swig of his wine and sat back in his chair.

"Well, one time, I went to Tuscany and bought a vineyard." He said casually.

"That sounds interesting," I responded.

Ok, the night so far was a big bummer, but that was impressive.

"It was....but... I lost it in my divorce. At least, I got to keep the restaurant. Now, I just stay put, enjoy my restaurant, and tinker around the island." He said with a little hope in his voice.

He was a weird man who did weird things and said even weirder stuff, but this was something I liked about him. He was local and wanted the island life precisely as I did. And I respected him for that.

"And here I was getting nervous thinking you were going to tell me about some sexual escapade you had last week," I said as I laughed a little.

Jack finally chuckled like a normal human being. Well, mission well done, Noelle!

"Well, there was... but...I don't kiss and tell, Noelle. This is a small island, you know." He said as he winked at me.

I could not help but blush. Despite his weird antics, he was still a very good-looking man who had his moves.

"I know, I know. I do actually have a very interesting romantic adventure to tell you about. I met this heart doctor on an airplane to Miami." I said as I started to tell a story.

"Sounds intriguing...continue," he said as he was some sort of a talk-show host interviewing his guest.

"So, I was seated next to a neurosurgeon from New York heading to Miami. We shared stories about our kids, home lives, and religious beliefs. We had a real connection," I said as I continued telling my story.

Jack shook his head as he gestured me to go one.

"Really, Noelle?" He said, his voice filled with amusement.

"Really, I know. My best friend, Lola, was a bit skeptical, and after two weeks of dating, she had him followed. It turned out he was not even a neurosurgeon. I said, remembering my naive little dating experience. I might as well be something of a creep magnet because this is the kind of guy I kept ending up with.

Jack laughed.

"You have to be careful, Noelle. Gigolos come in all shapes and sizes. Good thing Lola was looking out for you," he responded to my absurdity.

"We figured out he was just looking for a Sugar Momma." I laughed as I said the last part.

"Women are the same way. They are always looking for a Sugar Daddy. I just want someone to love me for me and my old, deflated balls." Jack said as he stared at me, making a puppy-dog face.

"I love your honesty," I said as I laughed. I laughed so hard that I spilled the sparkling water I was drinking on Jack's shirt.

Honestly, what is up with me today? Why could I not keep beverages in my mouth?

"Honesty, now that is my strong suit," Jack said as he flashed me his pearly white teeth.

"May all your days be so rich in color" Jack went on as he held his wine glass for a toast.

"And may all your days be full of the good kind of sugar," I said hesitantly. I wasn't really sure what to say.

"They already are, Noelle," Jack said as he looked deep into my eyes.

As we both finished our dinner, the waitress made her way up to us.

"Would either of you like some dessert?" She said as she looked at the both of us, one after the other, waiting for our response.

"Noelle, would you like something for dessert?" Jack said as he looked at me.

“I am good. Everything was lovely.” I said as I declined the offer. I didn’t have the worst time, but I also was in no mood to continue this night any further.

“We are finished,” Jack said to the waitress as a wave of disappointment took over him.

As Jack and I stood up, I saw that it took him a good second or two to gain his balance. It must have been the wine! He was clearly drunk. As I stood up from my seat, I was a little nervous that Jack might try and kiss me. To avoid anything like this from happening, I stole my gaze away from his, making sure I do not make any eye contact.

However, Jack clearly had other things planned in his mind as he walked over to me and made me look up when he planted a big kiss on my lips. Shocked is an understatement for how I felt at that moment.

Yep, I could not wait to be back home tonight.

“Thank you for a wonderful evening!” Jack said as he continued looking deep into my eyes.

“You are welcome. Good Night, Jack,” I said as I responded calmly. But I was not calm. What he did was not only bizarre but also uncalled for!

I was all for being spontaneous and passionate. Still, I was uncomfortable by this act, a little more than I was with his little stunt earlier tonight. I wanted to get out of there before he could get a chance to say anything else. So, I quickly said my goodbyes and took off.

I could notice the disappointment lurking over him, covering every inch of his face. Still, I left before he could say another word.

I quickly got home and settled in for the night. I started forgetting about what I had just experienced, snuggled into bed, and started recapping my time with Drew. Drew Darling. I quickly fell asleep with the sweetest dreams of what life would be like with Drew.

Chapter 15: Dinner Disaster

It had been less than 48 hours since my date with Jack Friday night, but I just couldn't help and think what a disaster it was. I mean, all I could think about the whole time was how Jack and I didn't have any connection at all.

Here I was getting ready for my second date with Drew... My, oh so charming, Drew!

There was something about him that made me smile. Just the thought of him gave me butterflies in my stomach. I had successfully spent all of my weekend daydreaming about Drew. It meant I was still not dressed when it was about time for our date. I knew I had to be quick if I wanted to look presentable.

I quickly changed into a gorgeous knee-length tea pink dress that fitted me like a glove. I wanted to put in a little more effort in my outfit because Friday, Drew had seen me in an entirely different getup, but tonight, I needed it to be different. I wanted to toss him a curveball. Especially after the "throwing-up" incident, Drew deserved a pretty date tonight.

After I finished touching up my hair, I picked up my phone to text Drew. But as luck would have it, he had already texted, "Drew: On my way, Gorgeous."

Even his texts were more electrifying than my entire date with Jack, but I was glad that was over. I don't have to think about it anymore. Thankfully, I didn't have to deal with Jack tonight.

Just as I was about to keep my phone inside the purse, my ears immediately picked up the sound of Drew's vehicle pulling up. I put on my coat that entirely concealed my dress and made my way down the stairs. I noticed that all three of my girls were watching TV. Good for me, I won't have to divert their attention from my date or me.

"Good Night, girls," I said as I rushed toward the main door.

I was so excited that I did not even tie the straps of my heels properly, but life wasn't fair. Of course, I had to wait a moment before I got to see Drew. Eva noticed me going out; she hopped off the couch and ran to me.

"Wait, Mom, why don't you have a gift for your date?" Eva asked as her eyes filled with intrigue. She looked at me from top to bottom, probably in search of a "gift" for my date.

"What?" I questioned Eva as I sit down to reach her height.

"Mom, you need to give him a gift. If you like someone, you give them a gift," Eva said it like it was the most obvious thing in the world.

"No...no...Eva, the boys give the girls a gift," I responded as I got up and kissed her forehead. I knew this was a long conversation, especially if it meant I had to explain to Eva, but I didn't want Drew to wait.

"Wait...wait, Mom, let me help you!" Eva squealed in her cheerful voice like she just had an idea.

"Ok, Eva," I responded with a chuckle. A spark of joy filled her. I was in a hurry, but I could not just leave before my daughter's mission was completed.

My eyes followed Eva as she skipped into the kitchen, bobbing excitedly. She looked for something when I saw her grab a flower out of the flower arrangement and open the kitchen drawer. With the flower still in her hand, Eva grabbed a pen, facial tissue, and tape.

I had absolutely no clue about when this little art project was going to end, so the only thing I could do was ask Drew to wait. Apparently, my daughter clearly was just as excited as me.

I slightly peaked my head out of the front door. There he was, with his eyes fixed to my door, expecting me to come any moment now. We made eye contact, and for a moment, his attractive, handsome face made me forget why I was out there. I quickly brought myself to reality and held up one finger indicating to him that I'll only need a minute.

Drew just nodded approvingly as he gave me his million-dollar smile. And I felt my heart beating out of my chest.

"Here, Mom! Here you go!" Eva said as she ran up toward me, swaying her small hands in the air. It compelled me to break eye contact with Drew.

She placed a flower gift-wrapped in a Kleenex tissue with tape in one hand and a chocolate candy in the other one. I could not help but smile at this adorable gesture by my little daughter. I bent down to kiss her on the cheek when I tasted chocolate.

"Oh, thank you, Eva. I see you had to sample the chocolate to make sure it is good enough for Drew." I said as I cleaned her face with the same Kleenex she had used to wrap Drew's gift in.

"Of course, Mom! Have fun!" Eva said as she licked her lips and stifled a cheeky little grin.

"You too, Sugar Bear," I responded as I hugged Eva and finally geared up to make my exit.

"Enjoy your dinner, Hot Momma!" Lola added as she slapped my ass. I was surrounded by people who expressed love weirdly, but I was grateful. I threw a flying kiss to the three of them. Finally, I headed out of the door.

I walked toward Drew's car, where he was sitting, waiting anxiously for me. He was humming along with the songs in his car, but he turned the music off when he saw me coming toward the car. Before I could open the door myself, Drew was already out of the car, standing by my side as he opened the door for me.

"Malady!" Drew said as he bowed down, almost forcing me to laugh.

"Thank you, Mr. Gentleman," I said as I smiled.

Damn, is there anything that this man wouldn't do? He's just perfect; I thought to myself as I sat in the car. He had indeed brought his A-game tonight.

"Hello, Gorgeous, so great to see you! Give Daddy some sugar!" Drew said as he almost ran to sit in his side of the car.

I raised one eyebrow. I was totally blown away by his enthusiasm. Drew was just so dreamy that I could not help but melt before I had time to say anything. I sensed Drew was already coming in for the kiss, and I more than happily welcomed it.

And to no one's surprise, we made out for a while. When we finally stopped kissing, I noticed Drew's face break into the biggest smile. But then again, I knew he had a similar view as me to not make any effort to hide reactions. I wanted him to know how happy he made me, and I was not going to lock any emotions away today.

"Oh, Drew Darling, you are so dreamy. Kiss me again, so I know I'm not dreaming." I said as I gazed into his eyes. I just could not get enough of him.

"The pleasure is all mine, Gorgeous." Drew looked into my eyes, making sure he didn't break eye contact. There is something about how he looked at me that made me feel like I was totally in love.

We started to kiss again. This time it lasted longer than before. I could feel myself getting more and more at ease with him with every passing second. As we continued to kiss, I felt the gift that Eva gave me fall down from my lap, so I broke away, even though I did not want to. Still, I had to before the chocolate melted, and my daughter's cute little gesture went to waste.

"My daughter suggested our date would go great if I gave you a gift. I tried explaining to her that it was customary for the man to give a gift." I said as I handed Drew the gift. I knew it wasn't any big gesture, but knowing Drew, I was sure he'd love it.

"WOW! What a mini romantic you have on your hands? How sweet!" Drew responded, flashing a smile. He did not take even one moment to open the gift I had just placed in his hands. He took out the chocolate bar and broke it into two pieces, handing me off it and keeping the rest in his mouth.

Even something as ordinary as this was dream-like with Drew.

"Delicious! Well, I do have a little something for you, as well." He said as he winked at me. Joy filled me, and I could not wait for what he had in store for me.

Drew reached into the backseat. His eyes were still fixed on mine. As he finally grabbed something, I could smell what it was. They were a dozen pink peonies, all beautiful to look at, blooming in their prime. I could almost die from the level of romance Drew created in only minutes.

"Oh, Drew Darling, they are gorgeous!" I answered as I smelled the peonies.

He was staring at me like he wanted to kiss me or maybe, I just needed another reason to kiss him. I reached his lips tenderly, lifting my right hand to caress his cheeks – his soft, plump cheeks, making sure I took my time with this kiss.

This kiss had to be the best of the lot...it was everything.

"Ok, let's feed you. I have a great restaurant for you! Do you like Italian?" Drew enquired, looking at the road this time.

"It's my favorite," I responded with a smile. How sweet of Drew to ask. Everything about him just keeps getting better and better.

As Drew started to drive, I couldn't help but stare at his perfect face, noticing every little feature, every curve of his lip. I didn't even bother looking out of the window to see where we were going because his face was so much more interesting. As long as I was with Drew, I could go to a restaurant that gave me food poisoning, and I wouldn't care. But before I knew it, we were already at the restaurant. As Drew parked the car, he leaned in to kiss me one more time, mesmerizing me more than I already was. Each kiss made me tempted for more, but we had to go inside and eat.

Drew hopped out of the car and walked towards me. He opened my door like the gentleman he was and stretched out his hand to hold mine. God, I felt good! I just couldn't help but continue to stare at his perfect face. I didn't even have the time to look at where we were. Nothing was more significant than Drew and me being together on this perfect evening.

"Oh, Mr. Jackson, so nice to see you. Your usual table?" the maître's voice sounded so familiar that it made me snap out of my thoughts.

I'm not sure what was exactly happening at that moment, but I know that this is the same restaurant where I was Friday night. But that wasn't even the strangest detail of the night. The fact that she called Drew Mr. Jackson was just as weird...something wasn't quite right.

"Wait? What? Mr. Jackson?" I reluctantly asked.

"Andrew Jackson Jr. is my full name. Are you ok, Ellie?" Drew responded. He must have sensed my nervousness because he started to read my facial expression.

"Yes, only a little confused," I said. I tried my best to put on a smile, but my voice came out like it was a little unsure of the answer.

"My dad owns it. Best Italian food and wine selection in town." Drew said, this time hoping his answer puts me at ease. But it didn't; it just made me more fidgety.

"Oh, so nice to see you again." The waitress from Friday night, the one that kept shooting me those bizarre facial expressions, said to me. But today, there were no odd looks, just a voice filled with amusement. My mind had slowly started to make sense of things, and it finally hit me.

Drew was Jack's son. I was speechless. I felt like my body could not move, but I tilted my face toward Drew to observe his facial expressions. He looked confused. I knew trouble awaited me.

"Have you been here before?" Drew asked as he turned toward me. This time, he was the one who sounded confused. But I did not know how to respond to his question. Should I just tell him, or should I lie? But before I could make up my mind with which way to go, I heard the waitress's voice from the background.

"Yes, she was here on Friday night with your father," She said, and I felt like disappearing, but I was not that lucky. I was still there, as visible as ever. I didn't want her to answer for me; that might as well be the last thing I wanted. I could almost not believe that she chose to answer for me. Remorse filled me.

"What? With my father? He said he was on a date with Noelle?" Drew exclaimed; his shock-filled voice occupied the entire area. I could almost hear the annoyance building in his voice.

The feeling of embarrassment started to creep up on me. My worst nightmares were nothing compared to what was happening tonight.

"My formal name is Noelle Edward. My friends call me Ellie," I said, trying my best to contain my anxiety.

But my discomfort was nothing compared to Drew's. His face looked like it was trying to make sense of the situation. He just slowly started to move away from me, retracing his steps and staring at me like I was a stranger.

"So, you were here on Friday night with my father?" Drew said. He didn't even bother to conceal the tone of disgust in his voice.

"Yes, but it was a horrible train wreck," I said, failing to keep my voice as steady as possible. The mish-mash of anger and embarrassment broiled through me.

I wanted to defend myself, but I knew the words I was saying did not have any meaning for Drew. He just continued to look at me. Maybe, he was making sense of everything, but his silence scared me.

The way he looked at me started making me restless. Every passing second, the feeling of aversion began taking over him.

"Kind of like this. You lied to me. You said you were going to bed. Instead, you were dating my father!" He said, finally breaking the silence. But this was the last thing I wanted him to say.

Drew looked disgusted. Emotions of being hurt and broken were visible at every inch of his face. But who could blame him?

He just had the biggest shock of his life, and if I was him, I probably would have felt the same way, but I could not risk losing what we had. I had to make an effort to make things better.

"Drew, stop. Let me explain." I pleaded. I stared at him. My eyes were searching his face for just a little consideration, but today was not my day.

"Stop what, NOELLE. Explain what? The reason why you lied to me!" Drew exclaimed; his voice was rising. He was pissed, and before I could say anything to change his mind, he left the restaurant. I couldn't do anything to stop him.

I noticed Drew rushing toward his car, his feet racing away from the restaurant. My eyes were fixed on him, but I could not call him. I did not even have the energy to yell his name. What would I even say to him? I'm sorry I went out with your father? Or that I was sorry I lied to him?

I noticed the faint outline of his body sitting inside the car. He smashed the car door as hard as he could, loud enough that I heard it all the way over here.

The fact that we had just came from that car happy and so into each other moments ago made my stomach turn upside down. And if all of this wasn't enough, I saw him throw the peonies out of the car window. This was it! What was supposed to be a wonderful second date turned out to be an absolute nightmare!

I knew this was my fault. I just wanted to make things better, but there was no way I could anymore.

I just stood there, not moving. I was trying to make sense of everything that just happened, but I couldn't the emotions overwhelmed me.

I could hardly believe that whatever happened here was real-life and not a scene from a movie. My mind was running wild with all my thoughts, but I knew I had to take a break, or else I would go insane. I had officially screwed it up with Drew.

Damn! Why did I not just cancel the date with Jack Friday night?

I tried my best to keep it together, but I knew I could not go home, not like this, at least. So, I decided to head to the bar and text Lola.

Me: I need you to come to Jackson's ASAP! It's an EMERGENCY!

She'd know what to do, and even if she didn't, she would at least say something that would help me. Just in a second, I heard my phone buzz. I couldn't be more thankful that Lola was a fast texter.

Lola: Yeah, I will be right there. What happened? Did you get your period or something?

Me: NO! Just get here!

I replied as I kept my phone down at the bar. I had to get a drink to calm my nerves.

Just as I was about to get another drink, I noticed Lola arrive at Jackson's. I still could not think straight, and the drink did not help me. If anything, it just made me feel worse about the whole ordeal, but I was glad that Lola is here. She gestured me to come to the car, and I obeyed. I wished to leave this horrible place. If it wasn't for stupid Jackson's, I would still be having a great time with Drew.

"Thank you! SOOO SOOO MUCH! What a fucked up night!" I exclaimed as I sat down inside the car. The nightmare was far from over, but at least I wasn't at that horrible place.

"What happened!" Lola enquired. Her face was filled with concern.

"Sooooo, Senior Sexy is Drew's father," I murmured. I didn't want to say it out loud because I knew how stupid it sounded.

"No Fucking Way!" Lola gasped as she covered her mouth. It was not every day that I saw Lola like this, but she was clearly stunned, but anyone would be. I mean, if this didn't happen with me, I would be just as shocked as her.

"Yes, fucking way!" I sighed, resting my head on the back of the car. I just wanted this night to be over with.

"Fuck, Ellie...." Lola said as she busted out laughing.

"...Ellie...Jack is my father..." Lola said as he mimicked Luke Skywalker. Even in a situation like this, Lola sure as hell knew how to lighten the mood. This is why I adored her, but even this couldn't make me see the brighter side of life.

"This isn't funny! We had so much chemistry." I said as I hit Lola on the shoulder. I just could not help but feel absolutely miserable. I mean, I was here a few moments ago, hoping for us to turn into something meaningful, but now, I ruined it. I absolutely ruined it!

Tears started to swell in my eyes, and when I couldn't hold them in any longer, I cried.

"Don't cry. It's ok. Let's go grab a glass of wine and talk." Lola said as she embraced me in a hug.

"Sounds good. Let's go to that cute little bistro in town." I responded. I was trying my best not to cry.

Quickly, I sat up straight, checked my reflection in the mirror, straightened my clothes, and took out the lipstick from my bag to retouch.

Who cared if I felt miserable? The least I could do is look cute!

Chapter 16: Dr. Bistro Bar

I closed my eyes, took off my heels, and placed both my feet on the dashboard. Lola hated it when I did that, but she didn't complain tonight. Just thinking about the date made my whole body stiffen up with angst; I could feel the creases forming on my dress. It was the same dress I had so carefully picked out for my date tonight with Drew. However, it turned out to be just like my date tonight, a disaster.

Driving with Lola was never less than an adventure. She drove faster than anyone I knew. She had her own logic that the time we lost while driving from one place to another is nothing more than a complete waste of time. So, it's better to be quick than careful. Logically, her thought process concerned me, but she was never the one to take suggestions.

She drove at the speed of light, so it didn't take us long to reach our destination – Pearl Street Bistro.

It was Lola's classic hangout spot. She called it the "Vortex Bar" because every time anyone of us got our hearts broken, this place fixed it. Even if we just wanted to get a drink or two, Lola would come here. They had the perfect variety of drinks that always made me feel better.

And boy, did I need a little pick me up after the date I had just had if we can even call it that.

Once Lola parked her car near the entrance, I got out of the car and fixed the creases that were now quite noticeable on my dress. "Don't worry about it. You always look hot," Lola reassured me as she started to head inside the bar.

"Yeah, it's not like I'm going to meet Mr. Prince Charming inside," I responded with a pout and followed Lola inside.

The Pearl Street Bistro had a scenic creek fireplace. The weather was just cold enough for the fire to add more than just appealing visuals to the place. The pathway heading inside the bar was illuminated with antique-looking bulbs, and the entire interior was covered with dark wood and leather chairs. It gave the bar a rustic laidback feel.

Lola stood near the long and narrow counter of the bar, and I stood near her, trying to find a place to sit.

"I don't think there are many places to sit here," I said a little loudly after I turned to look at Lola, who was already sitting comfortably on a chest-high stool placed directly in front of the bar.

"Ellie, there can never be a better spot in this bar than this one, or have I taught you nothing?" Lola questioned me. Her voice was muffled because of the noise of the blaring music and the chattering.

I laughed at her remark and sat down next to the one empty spot beside her. A guy was sitting only a few inches away. He was sitting so close that if I pressed my head a little back, our heads would clunk together. However, I couldn't scooch further away because the entire row was filled with people.

"We will have a bottle of your finest Stag's Leap," Lola said as she scanned the wine list for their selection of wines.

"Anything for you beautiful ladies." The bartender said as he winked at Lola and blew her a kiss. Lola looks at Ellie and smiles. "See, we got it, baby! Plenty of fish in the ocean, and we are remarkably close to water!" Lola said as she turned to face me.

However, I couldn't relocate my focus on Lola and her tales tonight. I really felt that Drew and I had something special, but here I was, sitting with Lola on a night that was supposed to be nothing less than magical. I was traumatized.

"I really fucked this one up," I complained. I felt like I would cry, putting my head in my hands.

"Let it go. If it's meant to be, he will forgive you, and this whole thing will work out." Lola was now holding both my hands and shaking me. However, I was in no mood to stop fretting anytime soon until we heard a third voice from behind me.

"Or maybe, it just wasn't meant to be," the man's voice intervened in between, which made both me and Lola jump.

I was pissed off; it's one thing to eavesdrop on someone, but jumping into their private conversation was a violation of privacy. The bartender was pouring their bottle of wine.

"Excuse me!" Lola exclaimed. She was pissed as she should be. Lola shifted my head to a little right. She wanted to look at the man that had just intervened in our very private conversation.

But suddenly, I saw her pause and giggle. Knowing Lola, I was a little confused. She was not one to shy from clapping back at someone, so I turned around to see the culprit. It was Futoshi, the handsome guy we had run into at the grocery store just a few weeks earlier.

"Sorry, I just thought you needed a second opinion," Futoshi said as he threw his hand in the air. It looked like he was surrendering to us.

"Oh, hey, wait a minute, aren't you Mika's husband? What are you doing here?" Lola asked. She had now moved her stool a little more to our side, and I could sense myself being sandwiched between the two.

"UMMMM no, she's my sister, and I live here. I am a doctor at the Hospital. My friends call me Yoshi." He said, clearly he wasn't impressed by Lola thinking he was married.

"You remember, Noelle?" Lola pointed toward me.

"My name is Noelle, but my friends call me Ellie," I responded with a smile. We were stuffed together, and there was not enough room to shake his hand, so I settled on a smile.

"Add whatever they are having to my check," Futoshi said as he called the bartender. Oh, wow! He was such a Mr. Big-heart, and I liked that.

"Heavy Son, you got it." The bartender responded as he began to make his way back to the bar shelf.

"Cool," Futoshi nodded.

"Doctor Money," Futoshi turned away from the Bartender and locked his eyes with mine. Weirdly, it felt amusing.

"Thank you, very generous of you. Investment in your evening?" Lola asks Futoshi, as intrigue was dripping from her tone. She was trying to hint at something, and I didn't pick it up, but Yoshi sure did.

"I enjoy spending time around a brilliant and charming woman. So yes, investment in my evening to keep you around." Futoshi responded suavely, and he was now smiling.

"Yoshi, is it?" I ask; I loved the ring to his name.

"Yes," he nodded his head in approval. He looked really cute doing that.

"Thank you, you are enchanting," I was being honest. His investment in our evening tonight really did help make me feel a little better. I was no longer thinking about the unfortunate situation I had been in, no less than 2 hours ago.

"Enchanting is what I was going for," Yoshi remarked with a smirk. He sure was quick on his feet.

"I will be right back," Lola said all of a sudden, getting up from her seat. I shifted my attention toward her, and she was smiling sneakily. That's when I understood that little miss Lola was only using the "bathroom" as an excuse to give us privacy. Maybe, that wasn't all bad. Yoshi was a charming gentleman, and I sure as hell did not mind being alone with him, so without any hesitation, I wave Lola goodbye.

I looked over at Futoshi, who had now moved even closer to me, our faces just inches apart. He was smiling at me, and I could just sense this miraculous connection building between the two of us.

"So yes, Cheers to tonight! Just a gentle reminder that what you seek is seeking you!"

A man of my taste, I see. I thought to myself as my lips involuntarily formed into a smile. Futoshi's words were a hint toward the conversation Lola and I were having earlier.

"You like quoting Rumi?" I enquire, my interest in him was building.

"Yes, and F. Scott Fitzgerald, occasionally, the Dalai Lama." Futoshi responded, "Drunk on the idea that love, only love, could heal our brokenness." He added to his already beautiful sentence by using a quote from F. Scott Fitzgerald.

"I love the words you speak. I believe in them, as well. Tell me more about your mind." I looked deep into Futoshi's eyes in an attempt to sneak a peek into his soul. He looked like a mystery. His brown eyes were no less than a magical quest that I wanted to embark upon.

This was the first time I looked at his face entirely, without any distractions. Futoshi's face looked like it was straight out of a magazine, every inch so perfectly shaped. His jawline was sharp to cut someone, and his choice of literature on top of that was just impressive. Everything about him was extraordinary!

The fireplace was crackling, and the laughter inside the place was almost deafening yet the conversation I was having was worth hearing.

"You are the finest, loveliest, tenderest, and most beautiful person I have ever known, and even that is an understatement." His eyes were filled with sparkle, and his words were flawless.

"Oh, I just love F. Scott Fitzgerald." I was gushing over him, I looked at his face again, and he was running a hand through his hair like he was thinking of the next thing to say.

"Can I see you again? Maybe dinner?" Yoshi finally spoke.

"Absolutely! Anything but Italian." My stomach clenched, and I shuddered just at the thought of it. After the experience I just had, I don't think I would ever be able to eat Italian again.

"Sure, let me put my number in." I obeyed almost quickly. I took out my phone, unlocked it with my finger, and handed it to him without even looking at it once. His eyes were a lot more interesting than whatever was on my screen. His eyes were locked on my phone, and his fingers were working quickly. It took him a little while to enter his number, but I could not complain. I had a pretty view for myself.

"May I have this dance, lovely?" Futoshi said as soon as he was done with entering his phone number. He placed my phone at the counter. He was now standing in front of me with his hands extended toward me, waiting for mine.

"Yes," I said willingly.

A slow song was now playing in the bar, and the noises of laughter and conversation were almost muted. It was as if Futoshi and I were all alone on another planet.

Chapter 17: Dawn of the Dead

Weeks had gone by since the incident at the restaurant with Drew. I had fought through my every urge to call him and think about him. But I had Futoshi to thank for it. Ever since our night at the bar, we had not stopped talking. I felt a real connection building with him, and I was no longer planning to change that anytime soon.

The more time that I spent with him, the more comfortable I felt. Yoshi was the only man that I was investing my time around, and I had no regrets. He was honest, genuine, and trustworthy. Of course, that perfect face of his was just enough to make any girl weak in her knees.

In the course of only a few weeks, the relationship we had formed was special. I felt happy after a long time, and it was all thanks to him.

Today, it was Eva's favorite day, the Day of the Dead. This year around, we were throwing a proper party for it at her request to celebrate Gramps.

I missed dad, and I was glad Eva had such a meaningful connection with him. She had specifically asked me to buy proper costumes for her this year because all her friends and their parents were going to join us.

I was sitting in the bathtub, soaking in the water and feeling it on my skin because I was exhausted after all the work Eva made me do for her party. "Mom, hurry up! My friends will arrive, and I want you to be ready." I heard Eva's voice ringing in the shower.

"Just give me two minutes, dear," I responded. The warm water on my skin felt nice. It made me feel relaxed, and I wanted to have just a few more seconds to myself. However, my daughter had other plans.

"Mom, hurry!" She screamed impatiently. Her voice filled with excitement was my cue to get my butt out of the bathtub at once. I knew if I was a second late, I would have her sad eyes to deal with. So, I quickly opened the drain and jumped out of the bathtub to get dressed. She was just like me, bossy and authoritative.

“Coming in two minutes, ma’am,” I said as I tied a bathrobe around my waist and walked out. I heard her giggling when I came into the room.

“Mom, look, here’s a present for you,” Eva shouted excitedly. There Eva stood; in her one hand, she held a hanger that had a dress. It was in a black cover-all and was touching the floor. She held a skull mask in her other hand.

“Wow, this is beautiful. I love it! Where’d you get it from?” I enquired, raising my eyebrows. It was a beautiful red, white, and black dress with a floral print.

“Futoshi and I got it for you yesterday afternoon when you fell asleep.” She said with her adorable little laugh. Her eyes were filled with sparkles.

“Thank you so much,” I bent down on my knees and kissed Eva. The noise of cars outside our house was Eva’s signal to leave the conversation as she ran off from my room at full speed.

I came out of my house dressed, wearing the long, floral Mexican dress that had frills on its side that Eva has just gifted me. I looked around to see the decorations. It all looked perfect. Simone and Lola had worked all night to decorate the house, and if I'm honest, it turned out pretty well.

The yard was decorated with skulls of all shapes and sizes. There were hats for all ages kept on a table, and the sweets were created with cane sugar. They were decorated with pieces of colored foil, icing, beads, and feathers. There were people all around; almost 20 parents and kids of all sizes were mingling, dressed up in Day of the Dead style costumes. Everyone around us looked happy.

“Job well done, you guys,” I called out to Simone and Lola, who were standing near the table taking pictures with Edward and Eva. Eva had painted Edward with black paint so that he could fit in well with the theme, and he just looked adorable. Lola and Simone were wearing multi-colored flowy dresses that had skeletons on them.

I slowly walked in the direction where the four of them were standing to see if Yoshi was there with them. However, he wasn’t.

"Eva, you look adorable," I said as I pinched her cheeks. She was wearing a hand painted mask and a skirt with multiple noodles on it. She had a headdress on, made out of red and pink roses.

"You don't look any less adorable, miss smokes," Lola said as she smacked my butt. My eyes popped out because of the sudden surprise, and it made all of us laugh.

"Hey, stop it! There are kids all around," I said, looking nearby to see if anyone had seen that. I was trying my best to contain my laughter.

"Oh ya, I forgot, Mr. Smokes is the only one who gets to do that now," Lola grinned with a wink.

"Speaking of Futoshi, have you seen him?" My eyes were in search of Futoshi. There were just so many people. The lawn was filled, but he was not one who my eyes could miss easily.

I was scanning around the yard when I heard Edward barking. "Who's bothering my sweet little child?" I thought, and I turned around to look at him. There, at the very end of the lawn, stood Futoshi with Edward. They were standing near a white picnic table that I had laid some snacks out on. Edward was barking intensely, and Futoshi was trying to make him leave. Futoshi took off the black hat he was wearing and threw it in the air like a Frisbee, but Edward did not stop barking. Futoshi would always deny it, but I knew he was a little scared of my fur baby. I couldn't help but laugh, but I had to help him.

"Throw him something to eat," I called out, and he quickly tossed some snacks at Edward. Edward being a good boy, quickly ran away in the direction of snacks. The two of them didn't get along too well, and it always made me laugh.

I ran over to Futoshi, and he kissed me straightaway. "Hey, where were you? I was looking all over for you." I whined. "I was here looking for you, my sweets." He responded, and we kissed one more time.

"Isn't this a good party?" I asked Futoshi.

"Any party with you in it is a good party," Futoshi responded, taking my hands in his. He was the smoothest talker, but his words always hit home.

I made my way over toward the table filled with photos of all our dead relatives, candles, and flowers. There it was, in a big ceramic photo frame, a picture of my dad smiling. Seeing him even in a picture was enough to bring tears to my eyes. I picked up his photo and hugged it slightly. I didn't want Futoshi to know I was crying, but perhaps he sensed it. He came up from behind me and wrapped me in a bear hug. I felt his chin resting on my shoulder, and his breath was hitting the back of my neck. I felt calm with him.

"Thank you for being here with me," I said, but Futoshi didn't say anything. He only kissed my shoulder and tightened his hands around mine.

The two of us just stood there in each other's company, looking at the sky and hearing the laughter that erupted on the lawn. Everyone was dancing around, having a great time.

Chapter 18: Bubble Bath

The roars of dusk started to howl in the tenebrous sky of the night, and everybody was draped in an aura of happiness. By around 9:00 pm, everyone started to leave the party. Edward was asleep by the fireplace, and Futoshi was seated on the cozy couch in the living room. Even from there, with a wine glass in his right hand, he couldn't take his eyes off me. At that moment, I understood what Futoshi has for me is not an infatuation but true love. I could discern the love he had for me in his worn eyes. I was blinded by the perplexity of not knowing if I am ready to offer the companionship Futoshi expected from me.

After seeing off the guests, sitting on the couch beside him, I appreciated the way life worked. It is something I will never be able to interpret. After all, life is nothing but an enigma. The way it abruptly starts maneuvering in your favor is beyond my comprehension.

"Come on now, Eva. Let's put you to bed," I thought in my mind as I grabbed my daughter from the carpet near the fireplace. I embraced my daughter in my arms and took her to her bedroom. "Sweet dreams, little one," I whispered in her ears as I laid beside her.

I came downstairs to pick up the house after putting Eva to bed. It was perturbingly quiet. However, I felt peace in this silence. I tied my hair into a ponytail, taking away their liberation.

Suddenly, I was blindfolded by someone. I panicked, but I settled quickly when I felt Futoshi's warm breath against my neck. "Trust me," he whispered. I released a pensive sigh and folded my arms together. He walked me upstairs and straight into a room. I could feel the coldness of bathroom tiles underneath my feet. His intentions became clear to me, and my cheeks flushed with a shade of red.

Futoshi slid the strap of my dress over my smooth shoulders and stripped me down. I was standing naked before him. He took the blindfold off my eyes and turned me toward him. There weren't any emotions on his face. Futoshi just stood there and kept looking me in the eyes. It felt like he was trying to look into my soul through them. I again folded my arms around me as he walked me into the bathtub. It was filled with warm water bubbles. He helped me in and played romantic music. Futoshi took out a lighter from his pocket and lit the purple scented candles that he had laid on the floor. Silence prevailed between the two of us. He walked closer, with a sponge in his hand, and sat beside the bathtub. I laid back, and Futoshi gently started squeezing water from a sponge on my shoulders. As I closed my eyes, I felt the warm touch of his lips on my neck.

Futoshi then unbuttoned his white button-down shirt and took it off. This discharged an abrupt rush of adrenaline down my spine. I watched him stand up as he unbuckled his pants and stripped in front of me. He possessed an impeccable body. I felt compelled by the vibe he gave off, and I wished nothing but him to embrace me in his strong arms. I tried to articulate words out of my lips, but nothing came out.

Suddenly, there was a scratch on the door that shook both of us. Needless to say, we both didn't give it much importance, knowing it was Edward who awoke from his nap. Futoshi joined me in the tub and kept staring at me. He took my hand in his hand and smiled. "I know it has only been a month, but I feel incredibly close to you."

I blushed, "I do, too."

"You see, I have never felt this way before," Futoshi added.

I didn't respond. Instead, I reached out to him and gave him a kiss on his cheeks, and rested my head on his chest.

"I need to tell you something, Ellie."

"Yes, what is it, Dr. Love?" I teased him.

"Ellie, seriously."

"Yes, what is it, Dr. Good Love?" I teased again.

Futoshi was offended, and he didn't reply after that. "Okay, seriously, my Dr. Sugar Cookie, what is it?" I smiled at him.

Suddenly, he pulled my feet using his legs and dragged me underwater. I was covered in bubbles when I slid back above. We both laughed at that.

"Well, I was going to tell you I love you, but you can forget that, my sweets!"

"Well, that's good because I have a 60-day rule on the 'love' word. So, even if you said it, I wouldn't be able to return the words," I chuckled.

"What are you talking about?" Futoshi was surprised.

"You know."

"You are killing me, women! Your rules are horrible!" Futoshi screamed jokingly.

"I know," I replied.

"I want you to be mine. I can't get enough of you, my sweets. My dreams are shaped around you," Futoshi confessed.

I wanted to get out of that conversation. Deep down, I knew there was more to it. I liked Futoshi, but a part of me still missed the comfort I felt around Drew. I missed him, but at that time, I didn't say it.

Futoshi was quite exotic when it came to making love. He held me tightly in his arm and started mumbling lyrics of a romantic song. It was cheesy, but I was blushing. He started kissing my neck again, then my lips, and then my entire body.

Chapter 19: Thanksgiving

I woke up with my head feeling a little heavy. I put my fingers on my temple. It was throbbing, and I felt like my vein would pop open. The wine bottle from last night was still placed on my nightstand, but it was completely empty. Had I really just finished an entire bottle all by myself? The episode that unfolded last evening had made me a little uneasy. I opened my phone to text everyone that the Thanksgiving dinner had been canceled, but I did not have the energy to expose my eyes to the bright screen of my phone.

Futoshi and I had planned a thanksgiving feast at our place. And if things were to go as planned, everyone would start showing up in ten minutes. Futoshi had taken it upon himself to invite our family and closest friends. Still, after what happened last night, I know that we didn't want to see each other for a little while. Not unless we talked it out! It was our first fight. Although it was barely a fight, it had left a bad taste in my mind.

Yesterday, Futoshi and I happened to visit the grocery store. He had suggested that we shop for the things we needed to get for the Thanksgiving dinner tonight. While we were picking up a bunch of grocery items, something weird had happened. I was wandering in the store searching for beetroots when I noticed a man near the vegetable aisle. I could not see who it was at first, but it looked like it was Drew from the contours of his body. I held my breath.

"Could it really be him?" I asked myself. This grocery store was miles away from where he lived, but it was him by some dumb luck. I was contemplating whether or not I should go up to him. After all, it had been more than two months since our "little incident" at the restaurant. Just like that, flashbacks from the night before started playing in front of my eyes. I didn't know what overtook me, and I began to stare at the man from a distance. I wanted to see him, but was it really the best idea to do so?

I just about geared up the energy to go say hi when a familiar voice interrupted me. It was Futoshi.

"Ellie darling, are you ok?" He said. He was sliding the trolley with his left hand while he placed his right hand on my shoulder.

I opened my mouth to respond, but I couldn't! I look back at the man standing ten feet away from me, but he was nowhere to be found.

"Uhm, can I help you, Ellie? You're freaking me out." Futoshi said politely. An expression of concern took over him, "Um, ya, actually – I thought I saw someone I knew..." I responded, being as discreet as possible.

"Oh, really? Who do you know that makes you so worried?" Futoshi's eyebrows were raised now. He didn't look concerned anymore, but I did not make much of it. I had more pressing issues to attend to.

"Who was it, Ellie?" Futoshi asked. The urgency in his voice finally brought me back to reality.

"It was Drew. Remember, the night we met, I told you abo-" He interrupted my sentence midway.

"Great! So, Drew is responsible for this mood of yours. What's wrong with you, Ellie?" Futoshi said frustratedly. He was holding back, saying something else.

"You know what, let's leave. We can just order all of this online. After all, there's no need to come here anymore." Futoshi said, and in a second, I felt his hand around my wrist. He did not care for my response. He did not even care that we had already bought half of the stuff. Futoshi just grabbed me and left the store. There was something about his behavior that made me feel wrong, but all of this took mere seconds before my brain comprehended what had happened.

We were standing in the parking lot when I shook my hand away from his grip. "What the hell was that, Futoshi?" I was confused, but the tone of my voice conveyed anger more than confusion.

"Nothing, I just don't think we should be there. I don't think he should see you. I don't like it," Futoshi said casually. He opened the door of the car and sat inside.

"You don't think? What makes you think you can tell me who I can and cannot see?" I snapped.

"Darling, don't cause a scene, just sit down. You're overreacting," Futoshi stretched his neck out from the window of the car.

"A SCENE!!! You literally just dragged me outside, and I'm the one causing the scene?" I started to walk away.

"Where are you going? Are you going to walk out on me because of that Drew guy?" Futoshi yelled back. He didn't even bother coming after me.

My heart was thudding in my chest as I walked away from the parking lot. I didn't want to be there any longer. Good for me if he didn't care; neither did I. It was almost evening, and the sun was on the brink of extinction when I opened my phone and called an Uber. "I can't believe this always happens with me," I sighed and booked a ride.

When I reached home, I had thought to see Futoshi there, worried or maybe even waiting to talk. However, I opened the door to an empty house. There was no one at home. Simone was out shopping for gifts, and Lola had a secret date, but nothing mattered right now. I walked toward my couch and sat down. I didn't know if what just happened was real life or a fragment of my imagination. I replayed the whole scene in my brain. "Was I overreacting the whole time?" I asked myself. Perhaps, I can message Futoshi myself and ask him about it. I opened my phone to text Futoshi when I noticed a message from him.

"When you're done being a drama queen, text me."

I was the one being a drama queen? Did he forget what he did no less than an hour ago? The message angered me more than it should have. I threw my phone across the couch and went to the fridge to take out a wine bottle. "I'll go to bed with you tonight, my friend," I said as I kissed my bottle of red wine.

I walked up the stairs and went to my bed. I popped open the new bottle of wine and started to chug on it, straight from the bottle. I couldn't be bothered to go down again and bring a glass.

I rested my head on the pillow and drank. I thought about how good everything between Futoshi and me was, but was I missing something?

It had been almost a month since Futoshi had confessed his love for me, and I thought everything between us was great. Ever since the bubble bath event, he had been acting a little weird, but I figured it was because he was fed up with waiting. In my mind, Futoshi was very understanding when I did not say it back.

The holidays were approaching, and I was afraid that season might bring a big gesture of love from him. For every time we met, he would continue pressing the I love you sign. Maybe, it could have been my behavior that fueled his anger, too. I had successfully avoided the much-dreaded conversation of where our relationship was headed. However, now that our 60 days were almost up, Futoshi's obsession was beginning to grow.

I adored Futoshi, and I enjoyed being with him, but was he really the right person for me?

"No, Ellie, it was only a silly argument. You can't break up with him." I was now having a full-blown conversation with myself. After a long time, I had found a man that was ready to be the man I had dreamt of, but maybe I wanted something to happen. Perhaps, somewhere deep down, I was looking for a reason to break up with him. Was I just making an issue out of nothing? I sipped another glass of my wine.

Was my mind still fixed on Drew, and this was all nothing more than the technicality I needed to call it off? I was going mad, but there was something about the way Drew had made me feel that, no matter how hard I tried, I kept my mind tracing back to him. Even after sixty days, I felt a sense of familiarity with him.

All these thoughts engulfed me, and I don't know when, but I fell asleep.

I didn't even know when Lola and Simone had come back home last night. I quickly got up to see where they were when my ears picked up on chatter coming from below.

"Oh crap, are they here already?" I started to climb down the stairs quietly when I saw my dining table filled with people.

I had not even cooked a meal, but everyone was already seated. Heck, I had not even seen what I looked like, but I'm pretty sure I looked like a chaotic mess, for every eye on the table was on me. The dining table was filled with food. My confusion was just growing, and I could see on the table Simone, Lola, Futoshi, Mika, and my other friends.

Why were they all here, and why hadn't anyone wake me up?

"Miss hostess. Good morning! How do you feel now, Ellie?" Simone asked. I was on the last step of the stairs.

"I'm ok?" I answered back, unknowingly. I didn't know what she meant by that.

"Here she is, the apple of my eyes. Sweets, I told everyone you were sick last night, so no one woke you up." Futoshi said lovingly as he saw me coming down the stairs. He walked up to me and kissed my hand.

"Sit down, my sweets. I saved you a seat right next to me." He took my hand and led me to the dining table. His touch reminded me of yesterday, and I flinched a little, but I did not say anything. I quietly just sat down. Maybe, today wasn't the perfect day to bring it all up.

"Come on! Leave the romance for the bedroom, you two. Let's dig in," Lola shouted with a pout, but I still was not sure why and how all of this had happened.

I felt so strange sitting in this group. I felt like I was an outsider that didn't belong there. I observed everyone's faces in the room. Everyone looked normal, especially Futoshi. He didn't even seem to remember anything from last night. Everyone bowed their head with a blessing, and then Futoshi stood up and carved the turkey. I could only think of one thing when I looked at him. What about the fight we had last night? Was it over so easily?

Chapter 20: Christmas Stroll

After the fight, there was not much to talk about with Futoshi. When I brought the argument up, he dismissed it completely. I asked him why he told everyone I was sick, but he didn't answer. The conversation was no better than staying silent, for Futoshi was adamant that he did nothing wrong. I felt a little odd bringing Drew up over and over again in conversation. Maybe, that was the problem.

Futoshi reassured me that it was not worth fighting over; he called it a trivial issue. I remember it was the night of Thanksgiving. He came up to me and took my hands in his hands, "My sweets, are we really going to fight because that Drew guy was in the supermarket at the same time? Not even once but twice? You know he doesn't care about you, but I do." And those words stuck with me. Drew did not care about me, and I supposed Futoshi was right. There was nothing left between Drew and me.

Perhaps, it was all in my head, and I was only trying to make a desperate attempt to see Drew.

I had spent days after the strange Thanksgiving dinner making sense of things. I tried to talk to Lola. Maybe, I needed to see it from a neutral person's perspective, but she reassured me. Talking to her made me think about a lot of things, like why should I think about him when he did not even have the courtesy to call or text me once after that night? He didn't even ask me if I reached home safely. For all he knew, I could've been dead that night. Ok, I mean, that was a bit extreme, but you know what I mean.

Ever since our little hiccup at the Thanksgiving dinner, I felt like I needed a little more time to adjust to him and his personality. Maybe, this was what he was like, and I just had to learn to grow with him. However, I didn't want to let Drew become the reason I ended things with Futoshi, so I just dropped it.

It was almost Christmas time. I could not spend my holidays screwing up my relationship over a guy that just did not care. I wanted to make my relationship with Futoshi work; maybe, he was right. I should not see Drew again. I held myself back from thinking about Drew. I sensed that Futoshi had started to get a little edgy whenever Drew's name was mentioned. It was best if I just dropped it.

I didn't plan on seeing him...but life had other plans.

Lola, Eva, and I were enjoying the festivities of the tree lighting and Christmas carolers. Futoshi was at the hospital as usual. Ironically, in some strange way, I was glad that he wasn't here. I wanted to have a chill night out with just my girl, like the old times. I tried to distract myself from boy troubles by using my entire holiday season in trying to get the perfect gift for everyone. I had tried my best to distract myself.

Eva was holding my hand, and she loved the time before Christmas. It was a tradition for all of us to go take a nice stroll, just a week before Christmas, and that's precisely what we were doing. The four of us were walking along the path of snowy filled streets when I heard her tiny, excited voice ringing in my ears. "Mom, Danny, and Curt! I'm going to go play with them." Eva ran off quickly after her friends Danny and Curt, and of course, as life would have it. Danny and Curt were with their Dads, Jack and Drew, the only father-son duo in the world that I had the absolute pleasure of dating. If awkward was a physical trait, everyone would be able to read its clear signs on my face. I was thinking about whether I should head over to the group when I noticed the two of them heading straight to us.

"So nice to see you all," Drew said. He looked at me. I could sense that it was directed to me. He had a very apparent look of despair on his face.

"Happy Holidays, Drew," I said as I looked at him. I gave him my best attempt at a fake smile.

"So nice to see you, Drew!" Lola squealed as she greeted Drew and then quickly walked over toward Jack and gave him a big hug. "So nice to see you too, Jack."

"Likewise, Lola." Jack smiled as he embraced her.

"Oh, you remembered," Lola said excitedly. Her face had an apparent glowing smile when she talked to Jack.

"How could I forget?" He responded, casting in that million-dollar smile he was always sporting. Jack was a delightful person, as long as he was not carrying a glass of wine in his hand. I shuddered just at the memory of that HORRIBLE date of ours. Yikes!

"Happy Holidays, nice to see you, as well," I said after thinking for a while.

Everyone looked happy. I was trying my best to be pleasant and act like everything was entirely normal. I looked at kids playing around with other children; it was a heartwarming sight. I noticed with the edge of my eyes that Drew looked uncomfortable. He was looking at me, but I quickly shifted my gaze.

Despite my attempt to completely dismiss his existence, I could sense him coming toward me. Drew walked up to me with a sense of urgency in his tone, and he whispered in my ear.

"Can I talk to you for a minute?" I was surprised by his directness.

"Sure," I responded. I was trying my best to play it cool, but inside, there were a million questions blooming in my mind. What could he want from me? Months later! I was visibly anxious.

"I just want you to know how sorry I am for overacting and leaving you that night at the restaurant." Drew's eyes looked a little wet, like he was holding back his tears.

"Thank you for your apology. It's fine," I said casually, but it was everything but fine. Yet, I wasn't ready to let him know that his behavior had affected me. I was about to leave when his voice stopped me dead in the tracks.

"I'm just really surprised after the connection I thought we had that you would be so unresponsive."

"Unresponsive, what do you mean?" I was quiet for several seconds, but then I asked him. I had always been here, waiting for him to call me, but he never did. How was I unresponsive?

"I've texted and called over 25 times," Drew said. He sounded irritated.

"I never got one call or text." I was being honest.

"Weird!" This did not make sense. How could it make sense that he called me 25 times, and I never got any one of them? In a moment, I pulled out my cell phone and saw that Drew's number had been blocked. I never blocked him, so who did?

"Well, that's actually weird," I said, finally gearing up the courage to speak. I was a little surprised that his number was blocked. Nothing made sense.

"What's weird?" Drew asked impatiently.

"My cell shows your number is blocked," I said as I moved my phone for him to see. As soon as Drew saw it, I hit unblock on my cell phone. I was still surprised that something like this could happen.

"Nice, Ellie." Drew was unamused. Perhaps, he thought that I had blocked him, and I was just covering it up with a lie. Whatever it was, I wanted to clear up the misunderstanding.

I was about to say something in my defense when I felt a familiar touch tap my shoulder. Someone walked up behind me and embraced me in a hug, and kissed my cheek. "Surprise, Love! I was able to leave early. I know you were waiting for your knight in shining armor to save you from being bored." Futoshi said once he wrapped his arms tightly around my waist.

I was startled and surprised at the sudden interference of Futoshi. It hit me in the face that I was standing in front of Drew, who he did not like AT ALL. But I wasn't doing anything wrong. We were just talking. I quickly turned around to face him and put my cell phone back in my pocket. I tilted my head to look at Drew, who was just standing there. His eyes were fixated on Futoshi's hands that were wrapped around my waist.

"Oh, Drew, this is Futoshi, Dr. Futoshi Fakumoto!" I said, somewhat embarrassed of his sudden intrusion.

"Pleasure," Drew's tone was cold.

Futoshi, without acknowledging Drew's existence, leaned over and planted a big kiss on my lips. After the kiss, I turned back toward Drew, who was not there anymore. He was already halfway across the way to the group.

"Did I interrupt something?" Futoshi asked. The loving demeanor that was present no longer than a minute ago had suddenly vanished. His expressions had changed drastically.

"Nope, nothing," I responded. I was about to suggest that we drop the conversation here before it escalated, but Futoshi had other plans.

"You know I don't like this Drew guy, then why are you adamant about talking to him, Ell, even after you know how I feel it makes me think-?" Futoshi's paused in between, but his questions did leave me a little shocked. I was not expecting him to burst out like this. His hands were on his waist, and his eyes were boiling with frenzy.

"Let's head back to the group," I said as I started to walk. How could he accuse me? But I did not want to fight… not here at least.

I was scared that if we had a fight here, Eva would see it, and I did not want that.

"I don't want you talking to him; I thought I made myself very clear last time." Futoshi's voice was now rising with every word he spoke.

"He's just a friend, Futoshi. I can't believe you're acting like this." I tried my best to control my anger. Why are we always in public when we argue?

"Yah, a "friend," sure, you know you're the one who is acting like a baby. He clearly doesn't care about you, ok? In case you need any help, he left you if you need a reminder. He did not even have the courtesy to call you? He's no friend of yours, Ellie. He doesn't even care about you." Futoshi headed back to the group, and he started talking to Jack about his arm. He did not care what I was feeling right now. He only wanted me to do what he thought was right, as usual. The word call made me remember what Drew had just said. He did call me; he said so himself. I needed to know what had happened.

I did care about Futoshi's flare-up, but he did not care about my feelings one bit. It was his judge-y tone and eyes that made me uncomfortable. I thought about going to him, but I wanted to complete my conversation with Drew, so I walked over to him.

"I need to tell you that I never got one message from you," I said louder this time, waiting for his expression to change.

"I can see you've been busy," Drew said. He did not want to talk to me, but I had to talk to him.

"Drew, you left me. You. Left. Me..." Futoshi's words flashed before my eyes as I said that.

"Ellie, everything happens for a reason. You clearly moved on, but it's ok. I will get over you."

"Get over me?" I didn't even know the words he just uttered were true or not.

"Gorgeous, I'm in love with you, but I can see you have moved on." I was confused. The three sentences that he said meant so much to me.

"Drew? Really?" I was curious, but one thing was for sure. The butterflies in my stomach had made a come-back.

"Yes, Gorgeous, I love you." He said, not holding back his emotions anymore.

"I don't know what to say," I responded. I was being honest. What do I say when someone I've adored for so long tells you that! But I was in a relationship. I was once more talking to Drew when Futoshi came in yet another time.

"Mind if I steal my girlfriend?" Futoshi came up from behind and gave me the biggest hug. He held my hand and took me away from where I was standing. I never knew what to expect with Futoshi. Maybe, this hug was his way of making me feel better, but it did not. For the second time, Futoshi was attempting to downplay the fact that we just had another argument. What unsettled me, though, was that how can someone, who was this upset, suddenly be so affectionate.

However, this PDA was not meant for me; it was meant for someone else. I know it had everything to do with Drew, for Futoshi wasn't even looking at me. He was only looking at Drew. If I didn't know better, it looked like Futoshi was showing me off like some trophy partner. Both that time and now, his love only peaked when Drew and others were there to witness his love. Was I just overthinking it?

Honestly, I'd rather be alone right now than be here. Life was strange. It always had ways to make you rethink every decision you make in your life. Right now, I didn't even know what I was doing. I locked my eyes with Drew, who was only staring at me helplessly. Things did not make sense for me at the moment.

Chapter 21: Sledding

When Futoshi dropped Eva and me back home, we didn't talk much the whole ride. He didn't even try and talk to me. In fact, as soon as I stepped out of the car, he drove off. Futoshi didn't even say good-bye. He seemed like he was in a hurry to get out of there. Perhaps, he just wanted to get away from me.

I could not understand Futoshi. I wanted him to tell me what bothered him. I wanted him to communicate his feelings to me, but he just wouldn't, not even when I asked. My head was running with millions of questions. What about what Drew had accused him of? Did Futoshi really block him on my phone? All of these questions made me anxious. I wanted to ask him, but I did not want to accuse him of anything that would just ruin everything even more.

What bothered me more than his strange behavior was his silence. Even when Eva asked Futoshi questions about his day, he remained silent. I couldn't help but think that he didn't want to answer them, that he didn't care about my daughter or me. It was as if he was an entirely different person when we were in front of people and a completely different person in front of me. First, I thought I was making it all up, but now, I was sure of it.

Futoshi would hug and kiss me, only when there was a gathering. But what about when we were alone? Did I not deserve love then? Being a boyfriend was not a part-time job, but he sure did think of it like that.

I recalled staring out the window of Futoshi's car. My eyes were scanning the clamors of Christmas lights and woods that flashed by. I was only thinking about one thing and only one thing – this relationship. I was embarrassed that I wanted him to talk to me.

But this time, I wasn't going to be the one who asked anything. I wasn't going to let Futoshi make me feel like I'm the one, "Making it all up in her head." If this is how he wanted to act like, so be it. I had other people in my life. He'll talk to me when he wants to.

My Christmas spirit by this time had been ruined. I wasn't thrilled or excited about Christmas anymore. Futoshi and I had not really talked since then. I had actually caved in once or twice and called him, but he did not pick up. I felt like a complete idiot. I was just scrambling, but it was evident that he did not want to talk to me.

This time, it was appropriate for me to feel sad. It was my first Christmas without my father.

Eva wanted to sled up and down the park, so I took her. No matter what happened in my life, I had all the time in the world for my daughter. We were having fun, going up and down the hill. And for a moment, I forgot all that was wrong with my world.

For me, it was just another one of those small town-hill, magical evenings. There were lights and a little airstream trailer/food truck that served hot cocoa. "Eva, would you like some hot cocoa?" I asked, getting up from the sled.

"Yes, I'd love some," She excitedly said as she took Edward's leash and wrapped it around her arm when Edward excitedly ran off. He was running into a crowd of people. Oops, I cry out loud. He was such a happy little dog.

"I'm so sorry!" I yelled, almost out of breath. I finally caught up with Edward and looked up to see the man Edward had crammed his body into. And as luck would have it, I found Drew and his son Curtis standing right there. Edward was hiding his face between his legs. I should have known. Edward doesn't like a lot of people, but he sure loved Drew!

"Oh, it's ok, boy! You're a good boy!" Drew bent down and petted Edward on his head. He seemed to enjoy it. I couldn't help but enjoy the cute little relationship the two of them shared. I looked at the three of them standing together. Their eyes were sparkling, and everyone looked happy, especially Eva. She was ecstatic to find her friend Curtis there.

"Mom, can I go down with Curt?" Eva looked at me with puppy eyes.

"Sure, Honey. Have fun!" I blew a flying-kiss to Eva.

"Want to grab a hot cocoa with me, Drew?" I invited Drew to come with me. I mean, who knows, we could try and become friends.

"Sure." He shrugged his shoulder and started to walk with me. I turned around to look at the kids; they were playing with the sled. I noticed Curt grabbing the tube and Edward following Eva and Curt up the hill.

"We will be right back with hot cocoa, kids," I said, waving at the kids.

"Mom, I want marshmallows in mine," Eva said excitedly. Her cheeks were all pink from running around so much.

"Ok, Doll. Ask Curt what he wants, as well," I turned toward Drew to see if he would accept my offer of getting hot cocoa for his son. However, Curt did not wait for his father's approval.

"I will take double marshmallows with extra whipped cream on top." He said as he licked his lips, just envisioning the delicious cup of hot cocoa.

"You got it, Curt! Two delicious hot cocoas coming right up!" I said to the kids.

The two of us headed over to the counter. I tried to look at Drew's face every little chance I got. I wanted to see what he was thinking. Was he going to talk, or was he still mad? We placed an order for four drinks and grabbed the hot cocoas.

"Let me hold them all," Drew said, taking away the cup holders from my hand. I was flattered.

No matter what happened between him and me, he had not forgotten how to be a gentleman. As we walked back, we found ourselves under a sea of lights. It looked beautiful, and the lights illuminated the entire passage. I looked up to appreciate the beauty of it when a snowflake fell on my nose. It was all just dream-like. My heart instantly felt better. I sipped my hot cocoa and had whipped cream on my nose. Drew leaned over and kissed it off my nose.

"Oh, my Drew!" I was speechless.

"I know I shouldn't have, but I couldn't resist myself," Drew said. He continued to look at me with his dreamy eyes.

"Did you like it?" Drew asked, hoping I was not mad, and I wasn't. I was just not expecting it.

"Yes." I could feel my face getting red. I felt guilty for enjoying it.

"Oh, Ellie, I've missed you terribly." His remark made my heart sing.

"I have missed you, too, Drew." I was honest.

"So, how serious is this thing with the Doctor?" I could see that he was dying to ask me this question. However, his question was not an easy one; even I did not know the correct answer to this.

"Honestly?" I asked. I did not know what I was going to tell him.

"Honestly," Drew said, not adding anything more to my question.

"I think he's in love with me." That was the only thing I could tell him right now. I remembered the day Futoshi told me that, but I don't think I believed it anymore.

"Of course, he is! But more importantly, how do you feel about him?" He raised his eyebrows in hopes of an answer.

"Well, honestly, I do like him, Drew. Futoshi, he is very nice and thoughtful but-" I paused in between. I did not want to tell him the whole scenario that happened a couple of days ago. Frankly, I felt a little bizarre, sharing my love-life troubles with him.

"But?" His eyes carried hope. He wanted me to say something that would give him some faith.

"Edward doesn't like him. Edward likes you better." I quickly think of something else to fill the quietness that my "but' had left. I did not want this meeting to be awkward.

"Well, dogs are excellent judges of character." He was smiling wide now as if he had just won some battle.

"I know, I know!" I said, nodding my head at his remark.

"So, when did you meet the doctor?" He asked, and I died a little internally. I was hoping this question would not come up. Because the answer was everything, but what he would want to hear!

"Um, the same night you left me at the restaurant," I replied hesitantly.

"Oh, I see!" Drew was visibly hurt.

I didn't know if he knew anything about it yet, but now he did.

"Drew, you left me over a little misunderstanding, then Lola picked me up, we went to that little bar on Pearl Street, and there he was. Before I knew it, he had my phone in his hands, putting in his number." It was not a great explanation, but I had to say something to defend myself. I did not want Drew to think that I gave up on our relationship. The whole night was nothing more than humiliating for me.

"I see." He said with a frown.

"You see what?" I didn't know what he was talking about.

"He was the one who blocked me."

"What?" I was confused. I could not think of how he made that connection, but somehow, he did.

"Don't you see, Ellie, I tried to reach you, and you never got my messages. He blocked me." Drew sounded pissed, but I could not blame him. Even I'd be pissed if someone did that with me. I had only once seen him this angry, and I don't want to remember that night.

I paused for a second or two. I was eyeing Drew warily. It all made sense now. That day, when Futoshi took my phone to add his number, he must have blocked him. I had to talk to Futoshi about it. I couldn't just leave it like that.

"Maybe, I guess." I managed to say finally.

"I want a second chance!" Drew said. His eyes were glimmering with hope.

"What!" I was a little shocked at how fast things escalated. I had to leave now before he said something more challenging.

"I'm serious. I want a second chance! Everything happens for a reason! I can't let you get away again." His heartfelt speech was interrupted as my cell phone chirped. It was a message from Futoshi.

I didn't know what to do or say. Out of all the days, Futoshi chose today to message me. I could not think straight, so I just continued to look at my cell phone.

"Or better yet, marry me, Gorgeous!" Drew's voice was as steady as a rock. I looked in his direction, and my mouth flung open. Drew was sitting down on one knee. I could not believe my eyes that this was happening. He was one hundred percent serious. I could not help but tear up. I know what I wanted to say, but I couldn't. I was with someone else right now.

I had dreamed my whole life for something this romantic to happen to me. Now, when the perfect man was standing there expressing his love to me, I did not know what to say. The whole situation was too much for me.

"Oh, Drew Darling," I looked away. I did not want to disappoint him, not right now. My heart was full of love after seeing his display of affection. But everything was disrupted when my cell phone rang again.

"I'm not going anywhere, Gorgeous. I am here for you. Take as much time as you need." He said, getting up from his one knee. Maybe, he was hurt that I did not answer straight away, but he hid it well.

I heard my phone chirp again. I looked into Drew's gorgeous eyes one more time, but I did not have the right words to say – at least not right now. I had to settle the situation before I got back to him.

"I'm going to go, Drew," I said. There was a looming sense of urgency in my tone like I was waiting to board a plane. I'm sure there were many better ways to leave, but I could not think of any right now. My mind was full.

I almost ran back to Eva. I probably looked silly to Drew, but right now, there were a few things I had to take care of. "Time to go, Eva. Nice seeing you, guys." I said, taking Eva's hand. She quickly ran to Edward and brought him where we were standing.

"Good night, Gorgeous," Drew said lovingly.

He had to stop doing that. Drew's voice was enough to make me want to run into his arms, but I had to focus. And I had to focus hard!

"Good Night, Evie!" Curtis said as I started to walk in the direction of my car.

"Good Night, Curtie Poo," Eva said, sticking her tongue out at Curtis.

I wanted to get out of there as fast as possible, not because I was uncomfortable with Drew's sudden proposal, but because I needed to know the truth. Before I made any decision, I had to talk to Futoshi once and for all.

Chapter 22: Christmas Day

The Christmas tree was lit up with all the presents underneath. Christmas this year was very different, at least for me. I could hear the sound of Christmas music playing in the background. This was my day to enjoy with the people I adored the most in the world, but that was not happening. I was a little beaten down, but I tried my best to put on a smile for Christmas.

I was sitting at my usual spot on the sofa when my attention floated in Lola's direction.

"...When loved ones are near, it's the most wonderful time of the year." Lola sang at the top of her lungs. She got up with her usual rush of adrenaline and took hold of Simone's hands. They both started to waltz in the middle of the living room, completely out of sync. I couldn't help but tease them.

"Hey, what if we're bad dancers? At least we have someone to dance with this Christmas." Lola winked at me as she spun Simone around.

"Ha Ha, very funny." I mocked her. I could see that she was trying her best to cheer me up, but I was not just in a very festive mood.

"Come on, Ell, you're breaking my heart like you've broken so many." She said, making a sad face. I know what she was referring to, and I just pouted. The only heart that was broken this Christmas was mine. I had so many plans for this year, but life rarely worked how I wanted to.

"Miss Ell, are you going to keep sulking in that corner?" Lola's words did not mean any harm. She barely even said something, but I could not help but think of the events that lead me here, sitting all alone on a Christmas night.

I walked to the dining table and picked up a plate. I only had one plan this Christmas, and it was to eat my feelings away. I filled my plate with cake and walked my way toward the couch, and slumped back down. Eva, who now stood on her tiptoes and joined in with them, was having the time of her life. My eyes were fixed on the three of them dancing and having a good time, but my mind was wandering. It was drifting somewhere else.

"Don't you dare walk away from me!" Futoshi's voice was filled with anger. Once again, his orders rang at the back of my mind. My relationship with Futoshi the night after sledding went down like a set of dominos. Everything fell one after another!

How could my soul feel happy if I refused to think about what caused me pain? I replayed the whole fight in my mind.

That night, after I dropped Eva home to Simone, I called Futoshi. I wanted to make things right; I hated this feeling of confusion clouding my mind. I pushed every thought I had about Drew at the back of my mind. Futoshi had texted me that he wanted to see me. It could not have come at a better time because I wanted to see him, too. I wanted to talk to him, and I had so many questions brewing in my mind.

One ring, two rings, but no answer! I called once again, and yet again, there was no response. Perhaps, he was busy at work. This time of the year was stressful at the hospital. So, I decided to leave him a message instead.

"Hey, Futoshi. Please call me when you're free. I need to talk to you." I typed the message and sent it. Not a minute later, I heard the sound of my notification go off.

"Can't call you right now. I have a few people over at my house. If you're finally free from your drama, you can come." I read his message, but I did not know what he meant by that. I felt a little rush of anger building inside of me, but I saved it for later.

"I'm coming." I wrote back.

"Sure..." with that, I hopped in the SUV and drove to Futoshi's house. As I turned my way around the corner where his house was, I could see that it was a little more than a few people. It was a full-fledged party. The Christmas lights on his house were already set and lit up. I tried not to let it fog my vision. I was here to talk about something a lot more critical.

As I parked my car and walked out of the car, I could see that maybe his house had a little too many people to talk about serious things. In any case, I had to speak to him. I got up the nerve and walked to the entrance of his house. I could see the people inside; there were just too many of them. Perhaps, it was in my best interest to call him outside. I grabbed my phone out of my back pocket and texted him.

"I'm here. Can you come outside?" I wrote, but I did not get a response. I waited for almost five minutes, and then when I started to walk back to my car, I fell a hand on my shoulder.

"I am here." Futoshi's familiar voice reached my ears.

"Oh, hi. Do you think you have a minute to talk to me?" I asked, making sure I wasn't raising my voice. I didn't want to sound like I was here for a fight.

"I have more than a minute, but not right now." He said, looking at me. I knew this was his tactic to avoid whatever I was here to say.

"Yes, but it's important, Futoshi. I think we should talk." I could not hold this conversation inside of me for any longer.

"And I think, whatever it is, can wait till after the party ends," Futoshi said, getting a little frustrated.

"You never want to talk, Futoshi. Something's always happening that restricts you from talking to me." I didn't care that I could not contain my anger anymore. I hated the fact that everything had to happen according to his timeline.

"Oh, come on. Don't start here. Now, can we please go inside? It's too cold," Futoshi said, clutching my arm tightly. It made me a little uncomfortable.

"I'm not starting anything, Futoshi. We're in a relationship. Why don't you get that? I think we have to talk," I didn't know why I had to plead to my boyfriend to talk to me.

"Oh, are we in a relationship?" Futoshi stopped dead in his tracks and turned around to look at me. I didn't know what he meant by that, so I looked at him with a puzzled look on my face.

"Ellie, stop the act, okay. I know you're clearly in love with Drew." Futoshi said, and I almost stopped him. It sounded odd to hear him say it.

"Listen to me. That's what I'm here to talk about." I said. I didn't want him to make sweeping judgments like that, but I had intended to ask him about the night we met.

"I knew it; it's always something with you," Futoshi said, rolling his eyes. I could see this fight was drifting somewhere else.

"Let me talk, Futoshi," I pleaded. Music from the house was louder than the volume of our voices.

"Yes, please do. But don't expect me to act like a nice guy once you're done talking." Futoshi sarcastically laughed like he was trying to suppress his anger inside of him.

"Did you block him on my phone?" I asked Futoshi with composure. I didn't know what I wanted to hear.

"What? Block who?" He looked a little shocked.

"Did you, or did you not block Drew on my phone the night we met?" I asked, making myself very clear. Futoshi didn't say anything for a while. Maybe, he was consulting in his mind what to say next.

"Please be honest, Futoshi?" I asked once more, hoping he would break his silence and put my mind to ease.

"Yes, I did block Drew. I'm glad I did, and you know why? Because you don't know what's good for you!" Futoshi finally managed to say.

The truth overwhelmed me. I could see myself getting distressed. This whole situation was getting too much for me.

I took a deep breath. I could feel my face reddening with anger. "And you do?" I asked what he meant by that. Futoshi was way out of line to do something like that.

"I was just looking out for you because you clearly can't," He said, trying to hold my hand, but I shook it away from his reach.

"Looking out for me? You didn't even know me back then. You had no right to do that." I responded, raising my voice. I didn't care that we were standing in the middle of the road and fighting.

"Oh, really, Ellie, you are the most immature person I've met in my life." Futoshi made sure to put stress on the word Immature.

It was happening all wrong. I wanted to cry. I wanted to shout at Futoshi, but I didn't. I had to stay calm and rational.

"What you did was very wrong, and if you can't see tha-" I got interrupted midsentence by Futoshi's booming voice. Everything about him looked great, but he was not the guy he showed me he was. He was a different man. He was a man that was so incredibly small that he did not care that he was hurting me. Here I was, standing in front of him, leaving Drew and his proposal stranded.

"Wrong? You can't even look out for yourself, Ellie. You have a daughter. You're a grown woman, and you act like a girl in high school." Futoshi didn't even think about the things he was saying. He was saying anything that came to his mind.

"Stop, Futoshi," I said.

"You wanted to talk, right. So, listen to me now. You need to stop acting like a baby." Futoshi said through gritted teeth.

"Please, Futoshi, stop saying all of this," I said. I didn't know how much more of this I could take.

"What is wrong with you, Ellie? You're a mess. I just wanted to help you, but-" I just turned around and started to leave. I could not manage to be here.

"Don't you dare walk away from me!" It was the last thing I heard him say, and with that, I left.

I know Futoshi would get mad, but this exchange was something else. I did not think he was capable of this behavior. I was angry and incredibly disturbed.

I could handle many things, but a statement like this from someone I called a boyfriend; never! I thought a lot of stuff about Futoshi, but I never thought he would turn out to be this guy. He tried to call me once or twice after that, but I blocked him.

When I finally came back to reality from the spiral of my thoughts, I sighed in relief. Thinking about all of this made my heart beat faster. After today, I had let go of all those memories, all those things that reminded me of that godforsaken day. I might be alone, but I was happy that I was not wasting my time fixing a relationship that was already broken.

Everything with Futoshi was history. I had to move on. I looked around to find the three of them talking about something privately. I felt a little rush of intrigue run over me, but I let it go. Eva was probably just asking about her presents.

I could see that Lola and Simone were spoiling Eva with more gifts. Eva started ripping into the rest of her Christmas presents. I was smiling, looking at them. Who cared if I didn't have Futoshi! Or if I fucked things up with Drew, the only guy that truly loved me. I wanted to go to him and apologize to him, but I was embarrassed. I did not want him to think he was an option for me. I don't even know if I deserved a guy like Drew. So, I just left it.

I left it all to fate. "Whatever happens, happens."

It was a while later – I don't know when, but I heard the door knock. All three of them, Eva, Lola, and Simone, looked at the door with amusement.

"Were we expecting someone?" I asked, but no one gave me a straight response.

"Looks like your Christmas present came early." Lola winked at me and walked to open the door. I did not know what she meant by that, but I knew that she did something. Her wicked little brain always worked in the most mysterious ways.

"Hey, what did you do, Lola? Oh, God?" I said almost in a high-pitched squeal.

"You'll see," Lola said as she pursed her lips together and swung the door open.

I stood there with my eyes fixed at the door. I was anticipating the arrival of this person that made Lola giddier than usual.

"I hope you like your Christmas present." I heard a familiar voice ringing in my ears. I immediately knew who it was. Butterflies flooded my stomach, and a smile was plastered on my face. The same beautiful face entered through the entrance of my home, holding a bouquet of stunning roses.

"You're here for me," I asked, fighting through my tears.

Drew nodded and ducked his head a bit in a shy manner. "Yeah, I kind of am in love with you, Gorgeous." At that moment, I pressed my lips against his. I could not wait anymore. I had waited so long for this, and when it finally happened, the moment felt surreal.

I chuckled, trying to contain my tears, "Oh, Drew Darling, I love you, too."

Chapter 23: The Kiss

Drew and I parked outside the restaurant, the same restaurant where everything went to hell the last time I was here. But hopefully, things were better this time. Ï could feel sensations of anxiety creeping up on me as I saw the name of the restaurant. If it were up to me, I would never come back here. This place evoked painful memories. I had no choice because apparently, something major had happened as her text read.

"SOS EMERGENCY COME TO JACKSON'S ASAP." And if I knew anything about Lola, it could either be something devastating or just nothing. Drew and I had our New Year's Eve night all planned together, but our plans changed once Lola texted me.

"I am so sorry for ruining our plans, I don't know what's up with her, but I hope everything is okay". I said as I looked at the flashing sign of the restaurant. The two of us were not sure what was happening, but Lola had messaged me to come to see her at Jackson's, and here we were.

Drew could sense that I was getting tensed. He could always tell by my facial expressions.

"Don't worry, Gorgeous. Nothing will go wrong this time." Drew squeezed my hand in his and looked into my eyes. Just one touch of his was enough to make me feel calm and relaxed. He gave me a confident look that everything would be fine. His striking gaze gave me much-needed assurance.

Ever since he showed up at Christmas, I could no longer ignore his love. No man had ever made me feel like he did. Drew and I had started seeing each other again, and this time we could not keep our hands off each other. There was something so peaceful and calming about his presence that I felt comfortable with him. I was the luckiest girl in the world.

If I was back at this dreadful place with someone else, I don't think I would even be able to stay here one moment, but this is what was so different about Drew. He made it his priority to always make me feel comfortable. This is why I loved him.

I was not afraid to say it anymore. I loved Drew.

Drew stopped the car, got out, and walked over to my side. "Gorgeous." He said, and we both laughed. It could not get better than this. Hopefully, things with Lola were okay too.

If not, I would not be afraid to say that this place was cursed.

Drew held my hand; his hands were so incredibly warm that I never wanted to let go of them. We started to walk together, hand in hand. Everything about this place was familiar, yet today, it all felt different. I was here back with Drew, but the atmosphere had changed. The feelings we both had for each other had grown stronger. The more steps I took, the more I could see how beautiful everything looked. The entire restaurant was draped with white sparkling lights. I was almost in seventh sky walking with him. Everything about this moment was nothing short of beautiful. I could not believe that just in a few days, my life completely changed.

I was admiring the beautiful decoration of the restaurant when I caught Lola and Jack in the middle of the restaurant, walking together without a care in the world. There was no one else there besides them.

The two of them stopped in the middle of their tracks and started looking into each other's eyes. Looking at the pair of them, my heart thumped loudly against my chest. Was everything ok? I was so caught up with everything that I had forgotten why I was here in the first place. The moment she sees me approaching her, she lifts up her left hand, and from almost a distance of ten feet away, I noticed a sparkling diamond ring on her ring finger. I looked at Drew and then back at her.

No one could miss the big, sparkling ring she was wearing on her finger. Did Lola just get engaged? I ran towards her in excitement.

"Oh my God! Lola and Jack. What is happening? How did this happen?" I shrieked in excitement. Lola held out her hand to show off her beautiful ring. It was magnificent.

Tall and striking, Jack was standing beside Lola, flashing his usual picture-perfect smile. He had his arm wrapped around her waist. "Oh, this has been going on for a while now," Jack said as he looked into Lola's eyes. I could tell from the way they looked at each other that they were happy.

A million questions popped up in my mind. Lola and Jack together? As ridiculous as it sounded, they were both just perfect for each other. I could have sworn I sensed some chemistry between the two, but I never knew they were this serious. I could feel my happiness growing ten-fold.

"When did this happen between you guys?" I took Lola's hand in my hands.

"Just an hour ago." She said as she kissed jack.

All the roller coaster of emotions I had just gone through were so worth this moment.

"I'm so happy for you, guys. I'm not even mad that no one told me." I said, trying my best not to cry.

At that moment, almost everyone important to us showed up. Danny ran up to the newly engaged couple and happily snuggled into them. Lola and Jack gave him the biggest hug. Everyone was just beaming at them, celebrating their happiness. There really was something incredibly magical about this moment.

"Look, Aunty Lola is engaged. She's going to get married very soon." I said as I saw the kids coming near us. Eva, Danny, and Curtis all hugged Lola and Jack one by one, their love pure and unconditional. It was an emotional moment to be together, sharing the happiness of the newly engaged couple.

"Once again, congratulations, you two!" Drew said as he hugged Jack.

"Thank you. We couldn't be happier!" Lola was beaming; her smile told us everything we needed to know.

"You'll be next, Ell?" Jack looked at Drew as soon as he said that, and my eyes followed him. I could sense my cheeks getting red with embarrassment.

"Someday Gorgeous. Someday." Drew said, kissing my cheek. A boyish grin overtook his face, and I couldn't help but stare at him.

Oh, his perfect beautiful face.

"As long as I'm with you, I am okay with whatever comes my way," I said. I meant every word of it. I loved Drew with all my heart, and as long as he was with me, everything was just perfect.

"They say immerse yourself in what you love." He took me by my hand and spun me around. This was the perfect night.

"Oh, Drew Darling..." His touch was the most soothing in the world. Being with him was like being in a dream.

"I don't want to be found. Ever." Drew embraced me in a hug. I felt elated; no one ever made me feel so special as he did.

"Me neither, Darling." Soft, romantic music played in the background, which abruptly stopped as everyone started looking at the big clock suspended from the beautiful deck of white lights.

"Just a couple of seconds more," Simone said excitedly. I looked at the clock and realized it is New Year's Eve. There was so much happening around us; it slipped my mind that we will be shortly joining in the New Year celebrations. And for the next few seconds, there was complete silence as the ten-second countdown came closer.

And it suddenly hit me that this was perhaps the right moment to kiss Drew. I was just waiting for the clock to strike twelve, so I could kiss my beloved.

Ten...nine...eight...seven, Drew and I continued to look into each other's eyes. Each second with him was enough for a lifetime. I could look at him all my life.

Six...five...four...with every passing second, my heartbeat was increasing. I could feel myself getting lost in the moment.

Three...Two...One.

He stared deep into my eyes and kissed me; it was tender. His lips were so gentle and soft that I wanted more; I could not have enough of him.

"Happy New Year Gorgeous, I hope I get to spend the rest of my life with you," Drew whispered into my ears and gently stroked my cheek with his one hand. With the other hand, he gripped my waist and pulled me closer to him.

"I love you, Drew, my Darling!" I cupped his face in my hands and kissed him. The moment was so sweet and magical that I wanted to close my eyes and hold on to it.

Tears of happiness welled in my eyes as I looked at him. Everything was perfect. I realized we were meant to be together - not for a lifetime - but for eternity.

Made in the USA
Middletown, DE
20 February 2022

61507945R00080